The Apostle's Apprentice

To Deanne + Dwight.
Enjoy the story

- Wayne

The Apostle's Apprentice

WP Gatley

Wesbrook Bay Books
Vancouver

Wesbrook Bay Books

www.wesbrookbay.com

Edited by Diane Tucker
Cover Design by Martin Buchan, Illuminati Designs
Interior Book Design by BDG LeGuin

The Apostle's Apprentice is a work of fiction. Although this is Biblically based, many of the names, characters, places, and incidents portrayed in the story are the product of the author's imagination or have been used fictitiously. Any resemblance to actual persons, living or dead, businesses or companies, events, or locales, is entirely coincidental, except as noted at the end of the book. To the extent that the image or images on the cover of this book depict a person or persons, such person or persons are merely models, and are not intended to portray any character or characters featured in the book.

Published in Vancouver, March 2016

ISBN: 978-1-928112-28-0

Contents

PART IV.
PART FOUR: MYSIA AND BITHYNIA

Acknowledgements

In the beginning were the words,

Then the critiquing: *thanks Scribblers*
Then the editing: *thanks Diane Tucker*
Then the publishing: *thanks Bev Greenwood and Wesbrook Bay Books.*

Then finally: *the manuscript that you shaped into a polished book.*

I can't thank you enough.
  –Wayne

Dedication

To all those who respect the wisdom and ways of Jesus.
He leads them and they follow because they are familiar with his voice.
John 10:5

Timothy's Journey

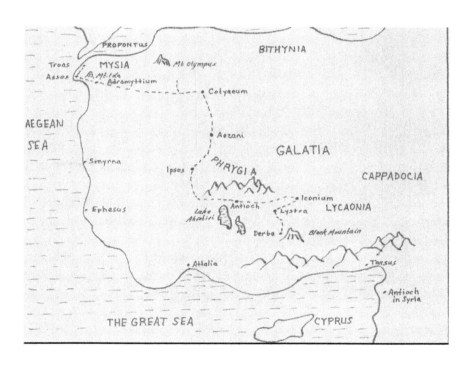

PART I

LYSTRA, A.D. 47

"*Follow the way of love.*" 1 Corinthians 14:1

I

Riot

NEDAR SCOWLED AT ME.

"I don't want your goat, young Timothy," he said. "You've spoiled him. There's more fat than meat on his bones."

"No, that's all winter coat, fluffed up from the cold," I said.

I knew Nedar's ways. Cheap as he was, he could be bargained with. "Remember last year. You got the best goat in Lystra, and it was mine. This one's even better. Only the greenest fodder over the winter."

I picked up my goat and shoved him onto Nedar's counter. I pointed to the sheepskin coat on his shelf. "I'll take that wool coat and two pairs of boots. Nothing less."

"You'll take a cuff on the head with my staff before I give you so much for that runt. Get away before I call a legionnaire, you thief." Nedar's words were harsh, but his fingers probed the kid's ribs and he couldn't stop his bushy eyebrows from shooting up.

Loud shouting and jeering came from the center of market square and we both glanced that way. When it stopped, Nedar looked at me with one eye partly closed and the start of a smile on his lips. "Your father, Andreas, he built my house, you know. And you, you're little older than a child."

That's when I knew I had him.

"Hah!" I shouted. "You want my goat. One pair of boots then. I won't be greedy. Put them aside with the coat and I'll collect them before market closes."

The jeering started again, but it was louder and angrier. I pushed the goat's tether into Nedar's hand and ran toward the shouting. I didn't want to miss this. There was always something exciting on market day and I wanted to be right in the middle of it.

I leapt over sacks of grain and olives, swerved around the butchers' chopping tables and stopped right beside Kopries. He couldn't walk. He was sitting in a chair near the stone wall that surrounded the market's deep well. Mother always gave him a few coins or vegetables from her garden.

"What's happening?" I asked. People were still shouting.

Kopries lifted his bony finger from his ragged cloak and pointed. The crowd were yelling at two men who stood on the wall, facing them. One was tall and brawny with brown hair and a beard. The other was short, with a black goatee.

"By the heavens!" I gasped. The men were our house guests, Paul and Barnabas. The people were yelling at them. Barnabas raised his arms. "Hear us!" he called, but even with his brawn and height, he was shouted down by the crowd.

What should I do? Stand up for our guests against the mob, or get away from the trouble they'd started, whatever it was?

"Lies!" someone in the pack yelled.

"Zeus is god of Lystra," cried another, "not some carpenter from a backwater village in Judea."

Everyone laughed. Someone shouted, "You would make a carpenter into a god? You're fools!" More laughter and jeers.

What would they think of me and my family when they learned that the men were living with us? I stepped away from the wall and tried to hide in the crowd. When I looked back, I saw Barnabas hold up his hands.

"Let Paul speak," he said. "Listen to our foolishness a little more."

An urge to defend my friends and a hope that maybe they would say something to please the crowd made me shout, "Yes! They're harmless. Listen to them."

People nearby stared at me. What had I done?

Kamilus, the baker called out, "Give them an ear. Can't do no harm."

A voice behind me shouted, "The boy's right. Listen to them. All in a day's pleasure."

Some of those who had walked away turned back. The rest shuffled about, but watched the two men on the wall.

Kopries still sat on his chair, not far from me. Should I take him away? He could get hurt if the crowd turned angry again.

Paul stepped to the edge of the wall. He caught my eye. I thought he looked grateful for what I had said. Then he raised both arms and in a strong, confident voice that carried over the noise of the crowd, he spoke.

"More than a carpenter." He said. "This man, Jesus, was born to a carpenter, true, but his deeds showed that he is God. He healed the eyes of the blind, fed the hungry and strengthened the legs of those who couldn't walk."

He looked at Kopries, who still sat right before him.

Kopries eyes widened, his mouth opened and he gasped as if he'd been struck by something. There was a soft murmuring among the crowd.

Paul paused and looked heavenward for a moment. Then he stepped down from the wall and reached out to Kopries.

"Stand up," Paul said.

The helpless man's weak arms slowly stretched from the folds of his garment until they met Paul's hands. Kopries' eyes closed and a soft sigh fell from his lips. Then his grip became firm. He struggled to his feet and tried to walk.

A hundred voices gasped.

Kopries held Paul's hands and stumbled for a few steps, then his gait steadied and he continued on his own. His eyes and mouth widened as he raised his arms above his head and turned about. He stared at his feet. Slowly, a broad smile spread across his face and his eyes shone.

I felt that my own feet were stuck in mud. I couldn't move but the crowd cheered, "Praise the gods! Great are the gods!" I joined in their shouts, rejoicing that a miracle had taken place in our ordinary town and in this god-abandoned age. It was here in Phrygia, centuries ago, that people had ignored the gods and the town had been destroyed by a flood.

These men, Paul and Barnabas, must be the gods. Finally Zeus and Hermes had returned to our simple city, forgiven our past wrongs, and performed a great healing. We had to give them the recognition they deserved.

"Zeus!" I yelled, pointing to Barnabas.

Others pointed to Paul and shouted, "Hermes!"

Paul looked confused. He turned to Barnabas who shook his head. People continued shouting and chanting the names of the gods. Even the Priests of Zeus, on their way to make offerings at the temple turned, fought through the crowd, and prepared to offer their oxen to Paul and Barnabas. Then I remembered that I'd walked with these gods that very morning and hadn't recognized them. They had every right to strike me dead for my ignorance. I collapsed to my knees.

The noise of the crowd was deafening. They pressed forward, bumped into me and trampled on my feet and hands. Through the dust and feet of the people around me, I saw one of the priests steady the ox while an assistant raised his massive hammer to knock the beast unconscious. Another priest had his sacrificial knife ready to spill the animal's blood at the gods' feet.

I scrambled up and saw that Paul and Barnabas were ripping their clothes to show grief and repentance. Paul shouted, "You must not do this. Stop! We are ordinary men, like you. We worship the true God and his son, Jesus, the promised one."

The crowd's clamor drowned out their words. Some Phrygians, who I knew couldn't understand Paul's Greek, howled the loudest for the gods to accept our worship.

The uproar went on so long I lost track of time until a loud voice cut through the din.

"You feeble minded peasants!"

Two men strode through the wildly cheering crowd. One was old Jonas, leader of our Hebrew community in Lystra. The other wore the prayer shawl of a rabbi. It was Shemuel, from Iconium. He raised his arms and called to the people to listen. "Don't believe this deceit," he railed. "These are not gods, but imposters, here to rob you of your common sense and trick you into worshipping them."

The rabbi marched over and spat on Paul.

I stared, horrified, as the spittle tricked down Paul's cheek and into his pointed goatee.

Shemuel's face shook as he shouted at Paul, "Liar! Imposter!"

Jonas leaned heavily on his walking stick and his thin lips twisted into a wicked grin.

Barnabas put his arm around his friend and wiped his face clean. I pushed forward to help, but Paul held up his hand to stop me. "No, Timothy, This isn't your battle."

The crowd had gone silent. Shemuel raised his arms and called out to them, "Don't believe this deceit. These men will rob you of your common sense and trick you into worshipping an executed criminal. They caused riots in Iconium and Antioch. They'll do the same here if you listen to their falsehoods and treachery!"

Someone shouted, "Stone them!" Other voices turned angry and people began pressing forward, shaking their fists.

A voice yelled, "Throw them from the city. They're not gods! Traitors!"

I shouted, as loudly as I could, "No! Listen to them," but the mob rushed forward and shoved me to the ground. I tasted the dust of the earth and stones cut my chin. My mind couldn't make sense of what I'd seen. Were Paul and Barnabas gods? They'd lived with us and shared our meals. Certainly they had strange beliefs, but people weren't stoned because they had different beliefs.

When I struggled to my knees a bony fist slammed into my head and knocked me back into the dirt. Someone pulled me to my feet. I caught a glimpse of the dark eyes and rough beard, smelled the cedar shavings on Father's apron. "Come away, Timothy. You'll be killed here." He dragged me away from the crowd to safety near a market stall.

As Father wiped my face clean with a cloth, I watched the mob turn on Paul and Barnabas. They beat them and hurled stones at Paul. They dragged him outside the city. My last view of the two men was through the city gate. Shouting, angry men shoved them down the small embankment next to the same road we'd travelled that morning. They lay like lifeless sacks of bones, stained with their own blood and covered in the dust of the streets their abusers had kicked at them. As I watched, Barnabas coughed and gripped his ribs. The other remained still. I thought he was dead.

Not gods, I thought. Gods would never submit to this. Emptiness settled in my heart. I took a deep breath. It came in shudders, and tears filled my eyes.

This was terribly wrong.

They were my friends and they needed help. I lunged toward Paul and Barnabas, but Father gripped my arm and held tight.

His eyes narrowed and his jaw set in his broad, grizzled face. "Stay, Timothy," he grunted. "This crowd is not done. Their anger will turn against any who help. Leave these men to their fate."

"But, Father, they're not bad men. They were with us at our home this morning. You were there. You know them. They were beaten only because of what they believe. It's not right."

He brushed his hands on his leather apron, then set them on his hips and faced me squarely. "Listen, son. Believe what you wish, but don't force others to believe the same or they'll turn on you."

Clouds had rolled in and covered the sun. It turned chilly and a thick mist began to surround us, masking the walls and rolling across the cobbles. I shivered and looked beyond the open gates at the two beaten men. As the thickening mist buried them, Father put his arm around me and we walked to the carpentry.

"Truth is revealed in layers," Father said as we lifted the heavy bar and swung the doors wide, opening the workspace to the market square. The mist followed us into the small room and the smell of wood dust failed to cheer me as it usually did. I wondered what Father meant, but was too miserable to speak. I picked up the plane from the workbench and tested it with a piece from the scrap pile, adjusted the blade and forced it into position with the wedge. Father picked up a burl of walnut the size of a child's stool and placed it on the bench.

"You'll learn that men are not simple, Timothy. Think of it as you shave this knotty round. Take a small slice with the setting of the blade and watch how the grain changes after each pass."

I imprisoned the burl in a vise. It was the shape of a turtle shell, sawn flat on top and mounded on the bottom.

As I worked, I watched the pattern of swirls and knots in the twisted wood and struggled to understand what malicious men had done to men of peace. Slowly, slice by slice, the smoothing blade revealed layers of swirling grain and each layer was more twisted and gnarly than the one before. How deep and mysterious were the patterns of people's deeds and beliefs. Jehovah? Zeus? Jesus? Was there not one single truth to resolve it all?

As I worked, Mother came to the shop with food and drink for a midday meal.

"My hard-working men," she said and put her arms around us. She lay her head on Father's shoulder, then stood on tiptoes to kiss me on the forehead.

"Your face is bruised. What happened, my sweet boy?"

"The riot in the market," I said. "I'm fine Mother. Don't worry."

She frowned at me, then cleared a space on the workbench and placed a wineskin, bread and cheese there. She held our hands as we stood before the table and prayed, "Blessed are you, O Lord, Our God, King of the Universe who creates the fruit of the vine and brings forth bread from the grasses of the earth."

Mother's slender fingers folded her headscarf around her neck and tucked the black hair behind her ears. Her hands moved in slow, graceful movements, like a grooming house cat. I dusted off the walnut burl and put it on the floor for her to sit on.

"That's pretty, Timothy," she said. "Beautiful patterns in the wood." She ran her fingers over its surface before sitting. Her dark eyes fastened on each of ours in turn. "I saw Kopries stand and walk this morning. I followed him through the crowd and spoke to him. Those men, Paul and Barnabas healed him. The people thought they were gods."

Father pulled a stool over and sat, then tore a piece of bread from the loaf and stuffed it in his mouth. I watched as I took a sip of wine. I'd never heard my parents discuss religion together. Father worshipped his household gods, as any Greek would and Mother worshipped Jehovah. It had been so all my life.

Mother rested her chin on her clasped hands. "The gift of healing is precious. Miraculous healing is only from God. I must know more, but how can I learn of this Jesus they preach, now they're cast out of our city, or dead?"

She dropped her hands and gripped Father's. "Might these men be the gods your people rejected centuries ago? You welcomed Paul and Barnabas into our home. Will you abandon them now?"

Father raised one eyebrow, tilted his head and waited for Mother to continue.

"Or," she said, "they may represent my God with new revelation of a great prophet, Jesus. Perhaps finally, my love, we may worship together. A new faith."

Father raised her hands to his lips and kissed them. He looked out into the market where crippled Kopries had stood and walked at Paul's command. "We'll talk tonight, I need time to think."

Mother nodded and turned toward the open shop front, touching my hand as she passed. "Listen to your heart my son. Faith doesn't come only from the mind."

She walked out into the market square and smiled as she pulled her headscarf up to shield herself from the cold and damp. She said she wanted to learn more, but I didn't know what to think. If these men were trouble in Iconium, they might also bring danger to us in Lystra.

I feared being on the wrong side of the mob and the rabbi but I had to hear more from Paul and Barnabas. They couldn't be gods or they would have struck their attackers dead rather than suffer their blows. So, they were men. Good men judging by what I'd seen. I had many questions, but the answers might soon be buried with Paul or leave with Barnabas who would surely never return to Lystra. As I worked on the burl, a sadness hung over me the rest of that day. Each cut of the plane seemed to bare tighter twists and darker grains. I couldn't shake a strong sense of injustice and loss. I was angry toward the mob and despaired of ever learning the truth. Even the coat and boots I retrieved from Nedar on the way home didn't brighten my mood.

After dinner that night, we reclined in the excedra, the open space below the bedrooms. The scent of our courtyard garden's windflowers and violets promised warmer weather to come. Father built a fire in the pit, but we still wrapped ourselves in blankets against the cool moist air. I longed for the comfortable heat of summer when I would discard the heavy cloaks of our highland winters. Stars twinkled above us through breaks in the clouds and a hazy moon shone, just over the eastern hills. Atop the barn, still against the moonlight, stood our windlass, a sheaf of wheat, to honor Demeter, goddess of the harvest.

"The grasses will green up soon, Father, and we can graze the animals in the fields."

"Soon, but not until a south wind stirs and the goddess turns north. Let the cattle finish the last of the winter fodder. See to it you muck out the stables tomorrow."

Mother looked up into the skies. "How I love this home. The heavens stretch over us like a blanket. Jehovah's been good to me."

Father turned onto his back. "The same stars hung in that sky when I bought this farm. It's been tough work wrestling fertile soil from the stony ground the gods allowed us."

"Andreas," Mother said, "I know you have little use for religion beyond your sacrifices and prayers. But I saw Kopries stand and walk, today. Isn't that certain proof of God's power?"

Father looked down at the fire and firmly shook his head. "Eunice, I've seen much trickery by sorcerers and magicians. Miracles alone will never convince me. You believe what you like and I'll believe in my gods. Just don't get us into trouble. That's all I ask."

Our donkey brayed in the stable and a groaning, shuffling noise just outside the courtyard startled me.

Father leapt to his feat. "Do you hear that?"

He motioned for us to stay back. As he walked across the courtyard, two beaten bodies stumbled through the entryway. There was Barnabas, supporting a bent and stumbling Paul, who raised his head, weakly, revealing a black bruise covering half his face.

I rushed to Paul's side. One eye was swollen shut and when I gently touched his bruised cheek, he recoiled and moaned. Father and I carried him to a couch in the *excedra* and laid him gently there.

Barnabas limped along with us and sat by Paul. "He looked dead all afternoon," he said. "Please help us, Andreas. It's not safe in Lystra. We have nowhere else to go."

Mother cleansed Paul's wounds and rubbed balm onto his injuries. It seemed there were no broken bones, but severe bruises, the worst of them on his face. Mother and I stayed by his bed and he woke often, complaining of a constant pounding in his head for which he found no relief. I slept little that night.

The next day, Paul rested in the open *excedra* facing our courtyard. Father went to Lystra to work and left me to help mother care for the men. I spent the morning feeding and watering our animals. By the time I finished with chores, the day was warm and the mewling sounds of contented creatures floated about our farm. While our pregnant ewe, Klara, chewed the hay with her cross-jaw bite, I nuzzled her warm musky wool, losing my worries in her luscious coat.

Then I took fresh stream water, bread and fruit and sat on a stool beside Paul. I held a cup to his lips. "The men who did this should be punished."

Paul sipped some water then raised his hand and weakly pushed it away. "Timothy, I don't blame the rabbis." He touched the bruise on his face. "I was once like them, arresting and imprisoning Jesus' followers. I hated them."

He paused to catch his breath. "Now, it is I who am despised," he said, gasping between words. "Yet Jesus' message is of peace. How can I get this truth to my Judean brothers?"

I avoided his gaze. He turned to Barnabas who sat next to him. "My partner in the gospel, answer me. How do I get past their suspicion?"

Barnabas took a damp cloth and held it to Paul's brow. "Be calm, my friend. Together, we'll find a way."

Paul gripped his companion's wrist. "But they're chained by falsehood. Their law imprisons them. They're far from Jehovah." He released his grip and dropped his arm to his side.

He turned to me. His eyes softened and he stroked my arm. "Timothy, you are young. Learn not to hate. Show only compassion. Jesus said that the law of the Jews depends on two things, to love God, and to love your neighbor as yourself."

Paul sighed. "The rabbis have forgotten this. But as for me, I resolve never to hate again. It hobbles reason and ruins lives."

The warm sun wrapped me like a blanket and my own eyes began to close as I sat beside Paul. Almost asleep, I heard, as if at a distance, a cart rumble on the road and a donkey bray. Our gate creaked wide and then my eyes snapped open. I stumbled to my feet and spun toward the entry.

There was Kamilus, the baker. He backed through our gate, tugging the reins of a donkey that pulled a two-wheeled cart. When they reached the courtyard, Heracles, the potter, jumped from the wagon and landed lightly on his feet. He whipped his long hair over his shoulders with a toss of his head. The cart rocked violently and

Kamilus planted his hefty feet to steady it and stop the donkey from bucking.

"Hold!" His powerful voice echoed through the courtyard, bringing Mother and Grandmother from the kitchen. The women placed their hands on their chests and sighed when they saw their friends.

Paul's eyes fluttered open and Barnabas called out as he gingerly rose from the couch. "Thank Jehovah you've come."

"We would have come earlier," Kamilus said. "We didn't know where you were and came here after searching everywhere." He turned to Mother. "Eunice, thank you for caring for our friends. Jehovah will bless you for your goodness." He bowed to Mother. "Now, we must take Paul and Barnabas away. They're not safe here."

Mother nodded. "I'll prepare food for the journey. Timothy, bring blankets and a sleeping mat. Be careful with Paul. He's still weak."

Heracles took Barnabas' arm. "The longer you stay, the more likely you'll be attacked again," Herakles said. "We'll help you gather your belongings and move Paul to the wagon."

I placed soft blankets and a sleeping mat in the bottom of the cart for Paul and packed everything carefully around him. By mid-afternoon, they were ready to leave.

Mother and Grandmother brought a basket of food and drink and gave it to Paul. He lifted his hands and held theirs. "Eunice, Lois, you've done what Jehovah asks of us all, to care for the stranger in your midst. His spirit is in you."

He closed his eyes and a deep crease crossed his brow. "Timothy, love even your enemies."

My enemies? I'd had none before Paul and Barnabas came.

We followed them as the cart squeaked its way along our deeply rutted road toward the mountains to the south. I felt a warm breeze in my face and turned to look at our wind-vane. Demeter faced north.

2

Wind of the Spirit

FATHER AND I HAD SWUNG THE SHOP'S DOORS WIDE TO LET IN THE BRIGHT spring sun, then he left me alone. I was cutting a piece of costly pine to length, focussed on keeping my saw blade perfectly vertical. When a figure blocked the light, I lifted the saw away from the wood and held it steady.

"Shalom, Timothy. Your mother told me I would find you here."

I cringed the moment I heard Jonas' voice. He and Rabbi Shemuel had started the riot against Paul and Barnabas.

He stepped through the scraps and curly shavings. One arthritic hand gripped his walking stick and the other rested for balance on the bench. Jonas was a devout Jew, elderly and respected in Lystra. Mother had been close friends with his wife until she'd died five years past.

"I was in Iconium last Sabbath and spoke with Rabbi Shemuel," he said. His fingers tapped the stick's handle. "I thought you might like to know what we talked about."

"Me? Why would I care, Jonas? My interests are carpentry and farming."

I once liked the old man, but his craving for detailed arguments over the law wasted my time and although I never saw him pick up even a pebble to throw, he might as well have beaten and stoned Paul and Barnabas himself.

A short white beard fringed his chin and when he lifted his head, it jutted straight at me.

"Jonas, you're standing in the light from the doorway. Would you move a step to your left?"

He shifted his weight onto the bench and sidled closer. He pointed his bony finger at me. "Rabbi Shemuel reminded me that you've not been circumcised. You must be, you know. You cannot be a Jew or marry one unless you are circumcised." He struck his stick onto the floor with a thud. "I agree with the rabbi."

"What? Circumcised!" I set the saw on the bench. "You must be out of your mind, Jonas. Am I an infant, to be circumcised? Besides, I'm Greek as well as Jew and I'm hardly the only one in Lystra that's Greek, Jewish and uncircumcised." Heat rose in my face. I stepped away and steadied my voice.

"I respect your knowledge, old man, but I won't be circumcised at my age. I do want to know the truth about God. Isn't that enough? Did you hear the teachers who healed Kopries?"

He stroked his beard. "Those men stayed at your home didn't they? What lies did they teach you?"

"None. They're good men, harmless."

Jonas spat through his teeth, "Harmless! They threaten the very basis of our faith. They're blasphemers."

My hands gripped the rough edge of the worktable and I bent toward Jonas. "Those two men healed a cripple but you stoned them and threw them out of Lystra. They were as gods among us, don't you see that?"

His eyes widened. His lips tightened and peeled back. He hissed, "Blasphemy! You bring God's curse upon this city." He gripped his stick and shook it in my face. "Rabbi Shemuel will hear of this."

I lifted my arms to protect myself from his stick just as Father stepped through the doorway and snatched Jonas' weapon from him.

"Leave here at once," Father said. "You would be wise to remember you're threatening a Roman citizen, old man. Don't bring your pompous attacks against my family or anyone under the protection of my roof. Now go!"

Jonas sputtered and nearly tripped over his walking-stick. He backed out the door with his eyes on me until he turned and stumped away, pounding his stick into the ground with each step.

Father leaned against the bench and put his hand on my shoulder. "And you, Timothy. I told you there'd be trouble." He held his hand up. "No! Say nothing 'til I'm finished. Mark my words, Jonas will not let this lie."

He picked up a chisel and stood by the bench, slapping its shaft against his calloused palm. The tightness softened around his dark eyes and his brawny shoulders relaxed. "I'm proud of you. You didn't let that troublemaker get the better of you. Jonas has no right to foam at you like a wild dog."

He ran his finger along the board I was cutting. "That old man is as dangerous as a viper in the dark. Beware of him. He'll stir this up until he's had the better of us. Mark my words."

I picked up the saw and examined the teeth. Not as sharp as Jonas tongue, I thought. "I'll be careful, Father."

That day we finished at the workshop early. Father put tools away as I swept the floor and scooped shavings into a basket, still thinking about my argument with Jonas. We stepped through the door into the sunshine, the sky blue and fresh. We closed and barred the doors, locking the darkness within.

I breathed in the cool air and felt an energy in my legs, the same anxious longing I used to feel when training for the games. I yearned to stretch out and fly along the hills and among the trees. "Father, I need to clear my thoughts. A run along the trails would help. Tell Mother I'll be late."

"Fine, Son. Be home by dark or she'll worry."

"Of course. I'll be hungry as a bear."

It was a perfect day to run, cool and clear. I started off slowly, heading south on the Roman road to Derbe. Where it turned east,

I left the road and began climbing a path I'd taken many times, winding up the slopes of the hills and into the woods. The lush green bushes and strong scent of pine and cypress cleansed the shop dust from my lungs and as I ran, my mind cleared.

I soon felt less troubled by Jonas. I knew that some people can't be satisfied, no matter how hard you try. Jonas was like that. If Paul and Barnabas hadn't come, he would have found some other excuse to attack me. I couldn't change what I was by birth, but I could fight for my right to be who I was.

A steep hill slowed me to a crawl. A small man ahead pushed a cart, leaning into it with all his strength. His black hair hung half way down his bare back. He wore only a dirty waistcloth. As I got closer, I saw that his skin was as grimy as his clothing.

"Greetings," I gasped. "I'm Timothy. What are you doing on the mountain so late in the day?"

"Sorry master," he blurted. "Sorry. I mean no harm. I do no wrong. Please don't tell me to the men, the city men. I go to my home. With the trees."

He kept his head bowed and peeked up at me in brief glances, careful not to hold my gaze. His hair covered his eyes so that he peeked through it or brushed it aside. His teeth were crooked and black, set in a face of high cheekbones and low brows.

"Be calm," I said, "I'm no threat to you. Who are you? I've never seen you."

"My name is Gurdi, master. I have seen you. You are the carpenter. Your father is Andreas, of Lystra. I know you. I saw you at market. You came with the gods. I have something for you. In my wagon. See, master?"

His voice was high-pitched with a heavy Lycaonian accent and distinct consonants that came quickly off the tongue.

"What's in your wagon, Gurdi?"

He reached in and lifted up a tunic. I took it and felt the worn cloth, spotted with dark crusty stains. It smelled of market dust and brought visions of the crowd, their angry shouts and the sickening thud of shod feet pounding human flesh. My eyes widened.

"See master. You know it. I see it in your eyes. It is the god's. I saw him in the market. He wore it. It is his."

"Yes, it is." I said. "How did it come to be yours, Gurdi?"

"Left in my wagon. We took the god away. We took him into Lystra and then to your house. The other god showed us the way. People in Lystra still angry about the gods. We took the hurt gods to your house in my wagon. We left him there. The gods went into your house. I saw them."

"Then you're a good man, Gurdi. We helped them get better and now they've gone."

"I'm sorry they have gone. Heracles helped us bring them to you. I work for Heracles. I take the pots he makes, big pots, to people. People give me food. People give me wine. I get water from the stream. You can hear the stream. Listen. You can hear it."

I closed my eyes to hear the reassuring gurgle of a nearby brook.

"Heracles had no pots for me today. He let me clean his shop. I am dirty from the dust in the shop. I will wash in the stream later. I met the cripple. Did you meet the cripple, Timothy?"

I could hardly keep myself from laughing. His ideas shifted faster than the turning of the mountain stream. He was like a dwarf in a comedy. Even his face looked like a theater mask.

"I saw him healed," I said, "but I haven't spoken with him. Tell me."

"His name is Kopries. He sat in the dirt with the dogs. He smelled. No one to clean him. He is better now. Kamilus, the baker, looks after him. First, Kopries cleaned the shop. Now he mixes flour and water. He gets strong and he sings. All the time he sings about the god, Jesus."

I had wondered what had happened to Kopries. I wanted to hear more, but I had to get home before sunset. "Gurdi, I must leave now. Come and see me at my fathers' shop sometime. I want to know more about Kopries. Will you come?"

"Yes, I will come, Timothy. You are my friend." A broad smile split his round face.

I left and made my way down the path, picking up my pace to hasten home in the fading twilight. When I reached the bottom of the hill, I inhaled the sweetness of clover and thistles in the grey dusk and sped along the familiar trail toward home.

Father and I worked in the shop again the next day. We opened the double doors and stepped into the cool shade. I loved the sight of the tools. Saws and hammers hung from pegs. Planes, chisels and blades sat on the shelves, each in their assigned place, like soldiers arrayed for a march. I breathed the fragrant citron-wood and earthy ebony, and the resinous dust of cedar. Father had collected only a few short lengths of these expensive woods, but their scents were unmistakable.

"These boards need smoothing, Timothy." Father held a piece about the width of my hand and the thickness of a finger. His weathered face tightened as he squinted along the length. He ran his palm over its surface. "It must be smooth as silk, my son."

My job was to prepare the pieces for a cedar table. It would be rubbed to an ox-blood finish, but with inlaid citron knots and an ebony meander around the edge. A wealthy merchant in Derbe had heard of Father's skill and commissioned the table. It was the finest piece of furniture he'd been asked to make and I was caught up in his enthusiasm. He ran his calloused fingers along the grain. "People will speak of me when they see this table. A man's life is only as eternal as the work he does. It lives after him."

"Like Caesar's conquests, Father? Praxiteles sculptures?" I asked. "But most men are forgotten, almost before they reach the grave. Yesterday, I met a man who surely lives unnoticed. His name is Gurdi. He keeps to himself and lives in the woods."

I picked up Father's drawings for the table. "I'd like to do something that lasts beyond this life," I said.

He wiped the dust from his hand and pointed to the plane that waited on the workbench. "Then get started, my son. Whatever you choose to do, give yourself fully to it. Then leave it to others to judge your work."

I'd learned to keep the blade sharp and adjusted very close to the base. Pressure on the tool's front at the start of the stroke and near the back for the finish made a smooth thin shaving. I was so intent that I was surprised to hear a whisper in my ear.

"Timothy, I've come. Come to see you and your father."

I knew from the voice that it was Gurdi. The little man's dark eyes sparkled.

"Gurdi, my friend. Bless you."

Father scowled at the curious intruder. He reached for our broom and strode toward Gurdi as if he might throw him out of the shop.

I stepped between them. "Father, this is my friend. I told you about him earlier."

He put the broom away and held out his hand. "Hello, Gurdi. Welcome the gods, my friend."

Gurdi took his hand. "Timothy said to come. I bring a friend. Timothy wanted to meet. You know my friend. You remember him?"

Gurdi went to the doorway and beckoned to a man waiting just outside the shop. His thin frame stepped inside and I recognized the sallow face in a head made small by the few, lonely strands of white hair rimming the back. He walked stiffly toward us, his hands a little out from his side for balance. It was the cripple healed by Paul.

I took Kopries' hand. "You're working for the baker, Kamilus, aren't you?" I asked.

"I am, yes, I am. He's very kind. He lets me bake the bread, but I've never worked before. I was crippled and Paul healed me. I must tell you, he healed me in the name of Jesus."

"I saw you healed," I said. "I was trampled by the crowd."

Father wiped his hands on the leather apron he wore over his tunic. "Kopries, I see you nearly every day. I never thought you would walk." He picked up our bag of food. "Timothy, we'll share with our guests and hear their story. I want to know if this miracle is real or a magician's trick."

We cleared a space on the floor, placed a cloth down and spread our bread, cheese and wine on it. The four of us sat there in the middle of the day and I was soon spellbound by Kopries' story.

He sat with his thin legs crossed and his back straight, like a sage instructing his learners.

"I remember that day, every minute," he said. "I had slept in the doorway of the baker's shop. My body ached and wouldn't move. I wanted to die and lose the pain forever. I didn't care if I ate another meal or saw another sunrise. I would just sit in the street and die. Kamilus opened before daybreak and took me inside. He was good to me that day. It gave me hope. I had never been inside his shop. Merchants didn't want me near. They think it hurts their business."

Father glanced at me and shifted his position on the floor. I'd heard Father say those same words in the past and felt ashamed of myself for ignoring this poor man. I began to realize how wretched his life had been. As he paused and drew a breath, he caught my eye. I saw a hint of sadness there, and pity for me. Why would he pity me? I lowered my eyes and Kopries continued.

"Kamilus lifted me onto a stool by the door and gave me some fresh bread from the oven. I'd never been treated so well and felt sorry about my thoughts of dying. I heard the noises in the market. Merchants argued and customers haggled over prices. From a corner that I couldn't see, came a different voice, a strong voice. 'Hear me!' it shouted. 'Come hear the master's voice. We bring a message of good news!'"

Kopries reached for the flagon we were sharing, drank and wiped his mouth. The lines around his eyes sharpened.

"Kamilus picked me up, with the stool, and carried me into the crowd. He sat me in front of a man with small eyes and a black goatee. He told me to listen to the man and that he had something for me.

A stray mutt with tight, curly fur limped into the shop, sniffed and thrust its grey nose into Gurdi's tunic. Gurdi held its jaw closed and turned it away. Father threw a piece of bread and the dog snatched it out of the air, then hobbled on its way. Dust specks floated in the sunbeams pouring through the doorway.

Kopries broke a fist-sized piece of bread and swallowed it with a slow draft of wine. He nodded his head as he spoke, as if keeping time to some inner music. "Kamilus hurried back to his shop. So sudden, so strange were his actions, I thought that I must hear this teacher. So I listened, and it's good that I did.

"The teacher looked straight at me. His eyes told me he knew I had no hope. All around me faded away. I heard only one voice and saw only one face, as if we were alone in that marketplace. I felt that something new was about to happen. He spoke of a man from Nazareth, Jesus, who made the lame to walk. I believed him. He called me to stand on my feet. I forgot I was crippled. He took my hand. My body strengthened. My legs held me up, though they hadn't since birth. Was I dreaming? I breathed deeply and it seemed that I took in a spirit of new life."

He laughed and pumped his arms. "I would never have to beg again. I would work and live well, like you."

He stood and clapped his hands. "A new man! Jesus didn't only heal my legs. He gave me new life. I bow at the goodness of God." Kopries lowered his eyes and opened his hands. He was silent for a moment. I held my breath.

Gurdi leapt to his feet and put his hands on Kopries' shoulders. "You see, Timothy. Was it not a miracle, Andreas? The gods did it. A miracle."

Father stood and rubbed his chin. He reached out and took Kopries' hands. "I cannot deny what I see before me. You're healed, Kopries. As to the cause of your healing, I cannot tell. I know Paul and Barnabas. They're not gods. They were beaten, almost to death. Gods don't suffer the beatings of mere men. No, this healing is a power from elsewhere."

Father scowled and slapped his apron. He pointed to the food scraps and grunted, "Clean this up, Timothy. And you, Kopries, what do *you* say about your healing?"

Kopries opened his hands and reached down toward his legs. "I was crippled and now I'm whole. In the name of Jesus, Paul healed me. I must worship the one who has such power and love. Jesus is my god. I feel his life within me."

Father put his arm around Kopries and led him out of the shop. "I'm glad for you, my friend. Come and see us again. As for me, if I ever need healing, I will come to you. But I am Greek, and Zeus is my god. Now, I can spare no more time for this."

I'd just finished putting the scraps in our bag and was sweeping the floor. Father stepped back into the shop and took the broom from me. "Timothy, we must get back to work."

"Yes, Father, just let me take leave of my friends." I stepped into the glaring sun and sneezed from the brightness. Kopries and Gurdi were waiting under the shade of the sycamore trees by the shop.

"Kopries," I said, "I must know. When you were telling your story, you looked at me with pity. Why would you feel sorry for me?"

His brows tightened and his eyes closed. He sighed and looked at me. "My friend, you are a cripple and I know what a hopeless life that is."

A cripple! My mouth opened. I gasped.

"Cripple," Gurdi bleated. "He is no cripple."

Gurdi danced about, pointing at me. "He has arms. He has legs. Timothy walks. He is no cripple. He is my friend."

Kopries looked at Gurdi and laughed. He turned to me, "Not a cripple in body. Crippled in spirit. Your mother told me of your doubt."

He reached out and held my hands. "Don't be angered by my words. Your spirit is weak, as my legs once were. It needs healing. Seek it. That's all I know. More, I must learn. Goodbye, my friend. I will see you again."

Stunned, I watched them turn and leave, my hands held out as if

Kopries were still grasping them. The comfort of his touch had left me when he released his grip.

They walked across the market square. One waddled with distinct care, hands out for balance. The other looked up at his friend while jabbering continuously, his dark hair flipping to and fro as he shuffled sideways beside Kopries.

3

Rachel's Choice

ON SABBATH MORNING I WENT WITH MOTHER TO WORSHIP AT THE RIVER with the Judeans of Lystra. Grey clouds covered the sky and the air lay heavy in the dim morning light. We gathered below an open hill where the river streamed behind us. The rabbi would soon take his place on the rise, beneath the dark tent, and open the holy scrolls that lay on a table there. There were not more than fifteen of us and only a handful were men: Jonas, his son-in-law Amram, and the metalsmiths Jotham and Hiram.

I'd just taken my place when Jonas limped to the front and turned to face the assembly. He glared at me and it brought back his angry words demanding I be circumcised. Sharp pain wrenched my stomach, as if something were tugging at my innards. I don't want to be here. Jonas' hateful stare made me feel like the worst of sinners.

My sense of shame increased when I saw Rabbi Shemuel. He embodied religious authority with his white-fringed prayer shawl and the full grey beard forming a halo around his weathered face. He was the most learned man I knew.

What I couldn't understand was his furious rejection of Paul and Barnabas on the day Kopries was healed. I hoped today's lesson would explain his actions. The fist gripped my stomach again.

He held up the rolled and sealed scroll, pressed it to his lips, and slowly placed it on the table. "There are some who stir up trouble by proclaiming a messiah." His voice rose with each sentence. "Such people are Hebrew in name only and do not speak the truth."

He pointed at Mother and me. "They are blasphemers and heretics. There is only one God! This Jesus they preach is an imposter! Any who follow such error will die in their falsehood, outside the faith. They are not welcome at these services."

A sudden wind stirred the wiry gray hair that hung loosely at his shoulders. He straightened his shawl and hissed his final words. "Those who are poisoned by the Jesus heresy must be shunned."

Mother gripped my arm. Her eyes widened and she put her hand to her mouth. Shunned? That would mean to be shut off from all Jews and barred from worship. She shook her head as Shemuel stepped to the side and Jonas completed the prayers.

I put my arm around Mother as a light rain began to fall, and led her away from the darkening hillside.

Jonas' daughter, Rachel, came across the wet grass toward us. She wore a grey *stola* with a blue shawl over her long black hair. She was ten years younger than Mother and a head taller, but the two had become close friends after Rachel's mother had died. Usually her bright, smiling eyes made me wish she had a younger sister, but now her brow was creased and her pale lips pressed thin.

She took Mother's hands and looked into her eyes. "Eunice, forgive my father's unkindness. I fear for your family."

Rachel glanced at her father and husband, talking with the rabbi just steps away. "Do you really believe what they say, that Jesus is the messiah? You'll be cut off and cast out of the faith and I'll lose you as a friend."

Before she could answer, Jonas stepped between them. His rodent-like eyes glared at Mother and he turned his back to her, facing Rachel. "Not another word, daughter. These are blasphemers. You are not to listen to them. Now come."

Rachel's husband, Amram, a small, dumpy man with a weak voice, stepped to her side and took her by the arm. "You stay away from my wife," he chirped at us. "You're worse than gentiles. Keep your ungodly ways far from my family."

As he dragged her up the riverbank, she turned, arm outstretched toward Mother who mouthed the word, "Later," and smiled at Rachel.

"When will that crusty old man stop?" I said. "Father warned him not to bother us. What can we do?"

In my anger, I hadn't noticed that tears marked the corners of Mother's eyes. She sniffed and wiped them away. "I'm sorry, Mother," I said. "You don't deserve this. You're the best among them."

"Amram has every right to take her away," she said. "He's her husband, after all, but Rachel is as a daughter to me. May it please God, I will speak to her when I can, privately.

"What'll you say? Do you believe Jesus is the messiah?"

I held her arm as we began walking up the wet bank. Mother tucked a few strands of graying hair beneath her headscarf. "I would believe," she said, "just to defy Jonas and Rabbi Shemuel, but how foolish that would be. They're wizened men, dried figs, trapped in their creeds and traditions. Their spirits are only dust and death. Still, to believe, I must be sure."

I was haunted by Kopries' accusation that my spirit was crippled. I saw it careening into a dark place, withered and dead in a dreadful grave beside the rabbi and Jonas. "What's dried up their spirits, Mother?"

She held her hands together. "Centuries of piling rules on rules, tradition on tradition have turned their spirits to stone. They're from Judea, Timothy, and strict. Our ancestors were from Babylon and not so rigid. Shemuel presses on us the unbending code of the Sadducces."

She stopped in a grove of sycamores where a crisp wind rustled the fresh leaves. "Their law allows no room for love." She reached up and touched my cheek. "My dear son, remember what Paul told us: 'Love the Lord your God, and your neighbor as yourself.' Jesus said all the law is met in that one command. These were also Moses' words. I believe them."

She looked at me and her pursed lips turned into a beaming grin. "I'll live according to this truth. Whatever I'm told that doesn't show love for God and others I won't do, even if the rabbi, himself, demands it. If that means I believe Jesus is Messiah, so be it. My spirit's been troubled over this, but now I'm resolved."

She raised her face to the cooling breeze and closed her eyes. When she opened them, she took my hands. "Your eyes are tight, my boy, and your mouth twisted like it used to be when you couldn't find your puppy."

"Tug?" I laughed. "That little mutt never could find his way home. And I never could keep my thoughts a secret from you, Mother. Yes, I'm confused. I'm torn within by Jonas' bitter attacks. I don't know the truth, but I can't be like him. I wish Paul and Barnabas were here to help."

I wanted my spirit to be free, but the faith of Jesus was too new for me to accept without knowing more. "I can't believe as you do, Mother, but I'll love my fellow man. Maybe in time, I'll understand."

Our route home took us north through Lystra. Mother lifted her skirt to keep the hem from dragging on the muddy road. Thunder rolled in the distant hills and travelers were few. Perhaps they'd taken shelter. As we walked through the city gate, Mother dropped a coin into the bag of the first beggar she saw. Many of them gathered inside the passage to get travelers' attention.

"I have no food," cried an old, toothless man in rags. Beside him a small man, his long hair bound like a black cat's tail reached into a basket and gave him a loaf of bread. Another man, taller and standing with his legs apart, gave the beggar a skin of wine. They prayed with him before moving on to another who waited with outstretched hand.

"Gurdi," I shouted as I crossed the street with Mother. "My friend!"

Gurdi turned and clasped his short arms around my waist. "Timothy. You're here. I am so happy."

Kopries called to Mother: "Eunice, my dear Eunice. I haven't seen you since the day I became whole. Thank you for the comfort you gave me. Of all in Lystra who saw me healed, you were the one who stayed with me in my happiness."

Mother held her hands up and Kopries took them in his slender fingers. He kissed them lightly and I saw the appreciation in her face. "Kopries, I was so happy for you. I had to share your blessing. What a pleasure to see you standing and walking."

Kopries hopped a few times, sending his thin hair flying. "I'll never forget the words you spoke that day. You said God had given me a great gift and I must live up to the trust that came with it. 'From those who have been given much, much will be expected.' I remember that. Bless you for your wisdom."

"And you're fulfilling that trust, working with Kamilus."

"I know these people's trouble and must do all I can for them. Kamilus and I bake extra bread for them. Gurdi collects the last of the wine from shops at the end of the day and Heracles gives skins so we can leave wine with people for their comfort overnight. We do this out of love for Jesus, and I to thank him for his healing."

Gurdi tugged at my elbow. "Come help, Timothy. Help us feed them."

There he stood, just half my height, tunic stained from work and sun-browned skin blemished with dirt. He could be taken for a beggar himself. Each day he cleaned Heracles' shop or delivered amphora of wine to inns and salvaged whatever he could. But that day he gave to others what he could have kept for himself. I wondered what would make a poor man give away the little he had.

"Today is our Sabbath, Gurdi. Our day of rest. Will you be here tomorrow?"

"Yes, come then. Tomorrow at sunset, we give the bread." He nodded, turned and went back to his work.

Mother took my arm, "Come, Timothy, they're busy and we must get home for Sabbath rest."

By the time we reached our farm, I'd decided to help Gurdi and Kopries. I still didn't know what to believe about Jesus, but my friends' kindness and goodness showed me a new way to live.

Each day, after work I distributed bread and wine to the poor. One day each week Mother brought goat cheese and vegetables. By the second week, she'd brought Rachel too, who became captivated by the idea of helping others.

"I hate that I have to hide this from my family," she told us. "It's so tense at our home. Whatever I say brings anger. Amram forbids me to leave the house except to go to market where I met Eunice yesterday. She told me what you're doing, so I came to see for myself. If this is what the Nazarene teaches, I must be part of it. But how can I defy my family?"

Gurdi spoke quickly. "The gods, Paul and Barnabas, were stoned for their belief. Paul was almost killed. Right there on that spot." Gurdi pointed beyond the gate. "They threw him through this gate. There. That's where he lay, dying."

He turned toward Rachel, his long hair flying. "Kopries walks now. You know him. You believe. I see it in your face. Stay, or go. You must choose."

Rachel paused. Her gaze darted from Gurdi to Mother then she nodded vaguely. "I must go home. They'll miss me. Pray for me."

She left without looking back and I wondered if she'd ever speak to us again.

The next day while we were feeding the poor, a chariot flew through the gate and raised a cloud of dust from the roadside dirt. I was surprised to see Rachel dodge to avoid the charging horses. As she walked briskly toward us, she glanced behind her. A white veil covered her face and her long black hair peeked from beneath a saffron scarf. As she neared, the delicate scent of lavender cut mercifully through the dust that filled my nostrils. We stopped and gathered around our friend. Her shoulders shook as she took Mother's hands. She took a deep breath.

"Amram has threatened me with divorce. He's gone to see Rabbi Shemuel. I'm not to see you except to tell you not to come to Sabbath worship. You're forbidden."

Mother's eyes widened. "Forbidden!"

Rachel held up her hands. "No, don't ask me to explain. I can't disobey Father. I fear what may come of it, but I can't deny my heart. Give me bread. Let me help." She took a basket and began to feed the beggars.

Mother's hands dropped to her waist. She turned from Rachel and faced us. "Well then, it's official. We can't join in Sabbath worship. What will we do?"

Heracles was crouched beside an old woman. He grunted as he lifted his robust body. He wiped dust from his beard. "Jesus rose from the dead on the first day of the week. We'll meet on that day and learn from one another."

"Yes," said Mother, loud enough for Rachel to hear, "and anyone who might just be at market could come. Where can we meet?"

"Out there," said Gurdi, and he pointed again to the spot where Paul had been left to die. "Where the god rose from the dead. We celebrate there."

4

Surrender

"THE WEST WALL'S LONG SHADOW RELIEVED US FROM THE DAY'S BAKING heat. Gurdi had brought extra flagons of weak wine. He knew our friends would be thirsty. The hungry huddled against the walls, listless and sweaty, nearly naked in their efforts to cool themselves. Yet, even the cooked earth would give up its warmth when the cold dark stole over Lystra. Soldiers would soon bar the heavy doors and send us on our way.

Mother and I knelt by a bone-thin beggar whose long, grey hair covered more of his body than the simple loincloth he wore.

He held his hands up as I put a loaf of bread in his spindly palms and set a wine skin at his side. "You're getting weaker, Therapon," I said. "Are you warm these nights?"

"Oh, yes," he whispered in a dry voice. He took a sip of wine, "I have my blanket and the nights have lost some chill. Bless you for your kindness." He broke a piece of loaf and chewed away at it with his few remaining teeth.

As I moved on, Mother straightened Therapon's blanket and held his hand as she prayed, "Lord, bless this soul and give him comfort this night."

Gurdi and Kopries were a few steps away tending to others. Few travelers entered Lystra so late in the day, but while we were busy, two men slipped in through the gate and watched us.

"Timothy, Eunice," they called.

I turned at the voices and saw their fringed tunics. The tall one's broad smile lit his round face and added sunshine to his full graying beard. The other raised his arms and I rushed to embrace the short man with the dark goatee.

"Paul," I shouted. "Barnabas!"

Gurdi and Kopries reached Paul before me. Gurdi fell to his knees and hugged Paul's legs. He pulled his long tail of black hair around and wiped the traveler's dusty feet with it, saying, "The gods have returned."

Mother held Barnabas' arm. "We've missed you."

Paul placed his hands on Gurdi's head and said, in a strong voice, "Rise, my friend. I am no god." He smiled. "But yes, I've come back."

He helped Gurdi to his feet and embraced him. "Don't put your faith in me, but in Jesus, the Son of God. I'm a man, like you."

"But I don't know this Jesus. I know you. You healed Kopries. You are a god." Gurdi stepped back and raised his hands toward Paul as though offering a gift. Tears marked a clean track down his dusty cheeks.

Paul grasped Gurdi's hands. "It was Jesus' power that healed Kopries. Will you follow him?"

"Yes, yes. His power healed Kopries? He looked away from Paul and his eyebrows tightened. He stared at the ground and his head turned left and right. "Teach me his ways."

Paul put his arms around Gurdi. "I knew I'd find faith when I returned. I've come back to fill you with the master's words and deeds."

I leapt up and shouted, "Thank you! I yearn for truth. We all do."

"Hallelujah," Barnabas rejoiced. "You bring ears to hear and we bring tales to tell."

He smiled at Mother. "Eunice, you cared for us in our worst days.

Are we still welcome at your home, or have we caused too much trouble?"

"Yes, there's been trouble, Barnabas, but you're welcome. We have so many questions."

Mother turned to the others, "Everyone come! Come to our farm. We'll celebrate that these good men have come back. They can start teaching this very night."

Kopries walked beside Barnabas and told the story of his healing. The apostle listened carefully, as if he hadn't witnessed the miracle himself. He laughed easily and held Kopries' arm while asking questions. "How did you feel when Paul reached out to you? What did you think as your legs healed?" All the time, he made sure the rest of us heard Kopries' words. He saw me watching and winked at me.

That made me feel like he was my best friend, that I could trust him with my secrets. He was a backwater eddy in a quickly moving stream, gracefully drawing everyone into his circle of affection.

Kopries' story ended and we walked in silence.

I moved closer to Barnabas. "Why did you come back?" I asked. "You know you could be killed by the Judean leaders."

Barnabas gave my shoulder a light squeeze. "What about you, Timothy? What do you believe? That's what matters."

The final rim of sun dropped below the hills and left an orange glow. I slowed to think about my friend's question as I watched the silhouettes of Kopries, Mother, and Gurdi climbing the hill toward the farmhouse.

"Father worships Zeus," I said, "and Mother now follows Jesus. I don't know what to believe. I know you and Paul are honest and truthful men. I know that what I saw in the market was a miracle."

I shrugged. "I've decided to do as Jesus taught. I'll love God and my fellow man. But I won't cause trouble in our village. There's too much tension between Judeans and believers. I don't want to add to that."

Barnabas stopped. "Timothy, you can spend the rest of your life here in Lystra. Help the poor, listen to the truth, meet with believers.

Do all the good you want. You'll be respected. You'll be safe. But to follow only the messiah's gentlest teaching, to protect yourself, is cowardly."

I stepped out of his grasp. I wanted to defend myself, but I knew he was right. "Do you think I'm living a selfish life?"

His eyes sparkled. "Timothy, my one ambition in life is to tell people the good news of peace with God. Ask yourself, what's your purpose? He's calling you, my friend."

"I see that you and Paul have a mighty goal," I said. "Your lives are dedicated to changing people and giving them hope. I'd like more purpose in my life, but how's that possible for a simple villager?"

Barnabas' eyes narrowed. "Until I surrendered to Jesus, I was only a rebellious prodigal. Then I made him my master. I followed him even though it was dangerous. Nothing less will do. You must decide."

When I heard the word surrendered, I felt a sense of release and clarity. To whom would I surrender? Who would I follow? Those were the questions that mattered.

A flickering glow from the lantern in our courtyard fought bravely against the starry night. Barnabas walked toward the farm and I looked to the dark skies above. My gaze fixed on the evening star, its lonely light holding out against the heavens' vast darkness. I remembered Shemuel banishing Mother and Jonas harassing Rachel. Father's gods demanded offerings and servility but returned nothing to the devotee. I realized that I had already turned my back on those beliefs.

Only one faith shone in the darkness.

What Messiah was doing through his followers was changing Lystra. My future came down to this simple choice: surrender to Jesus, or serve myself. I ran to the gate and gripped Barnabas' arm. "Barnabas, I'm with you. Your cause is mine. I will follow Jesus."

He put his great arms around me. "My brother," he said. "Messiah told us to go to all the world and be a light in every nation. It's a great thing you've decided. A mighty adventure awaits you!"

Faith had come slowly to me, a breeze that first rustled the leaves then swayed the branches in the forest of my mind. Now, the patient zephyr had stirred again and spoken boldly to my soul, "Jesus is the way, his truth is certain."

At the farm, we set up tables and food in the courtyard. Father arrived a little later. Mother greeted him and whispered in his ear, pointing to our gathering. Father stepped forward. He clapped his hands and raised his arms above his head. He stood large before us with his lips tightly pressed and deep furrows between his brows. Everyone stopped talking and turned to face him.

He pointed to Barnabas and Paul. "You brought trouble to this little village," he said. "There are some who won't speak to me or do business with me. My son is confused about religion. My wife can't talk to her Judean friends or attend their services."

He paused and a smile spread across his face. "But I'm always prepared for an honorable battle. I despise pious, rigid ways, but I see the noble things you do. I give you permission to meet in this courtyard whenever you wish, so long as you don't expect me to believe your preaching. I don't need another god, I have plenty already."

He turned to Mother and put his arm around her. "These friends of yours are talked about throughout the village. Everyone has noticed their kind deeds. Feed them well tonight. I'll bring wine and butcher a young goat. Let's feast the return of these virtuous men, Paul and Barnabas!"

He called me, "Timothy, come and help me with the goat."

"Of course, Father." We left the courtyard and went to the stables. He pointed to a kid, probably four months old.

"That one," he said.

"Very well." As I tied a rope around the goat's neck, I asked, "I don't understand why you're so friendly to Paul and Barnabas. You don't believe in their god and they cause you trouble with the Judeans."

"You're right. I don't believe, and they are trouble for me. But they're changing this village and the people in it. They're doing more good than I've ever seen in one place. If this continues, the world will be a kinder, more peaceful place. So let's feast and work like them. Maybe they'll even save you from your confusion."

"Confusion? No, no. I've decided to follow Jesus, the Nazarene. I've found the truth."

"I thought you would." Father held his knife up to the kid's neck. "Perhaps my gods are old and tired. Time for change." He pulled the sharp blade across the animal's throat and I watched the life go out of its eyes. "You keep in mind what is good and right, whatever else you're taught. I see the decency in these men. If you live like them, the good you do will overcome much evil."

Father roasted the goat over an open fire in the courtyard. We dipped each piece into the thick soured milk that Grandmother brought. Mother set out bowls of olives, apples and grapes. Father brought an amphora of local wine, sweet and strong. The courtyard was lit with torches. The evening star and its companions provided a glorious canopy above. If there is a heaven, I thought, this is it.

Father made quite a show of pouring each goblet. "Drink hearty, followers of Jesus," he said, His curly hair shook and his beard bobbed with enthusiasm. "You'll need courage and spirit to change the world. Find some in this wine."

Kopries stood in the firelight like a sapling, arms hanging a little apart from his sides. He danced gracefully, without the clumsiness of the first days after he was healed. He chanted, "The lame man walks, the blind man sees. The mercy of God is seen in me."

I stood and took his hand. We pranced together around the fire. Paul, Barnabas and Gurdi sang in chorus. Grandmother lifted a sprightly foot and Mother pulled Father from his stool. He joined in the revels, even singing songs with us. As we tired, our voices died and we stood and watched the flames shrink.

Grandmother heaved a great sigh, "That's quite enough for me. Time for my warm sheepskin blanket." She walked slowly to the house, holding her back with one hand and stretching the other out for balance. Father took her hand and helped her up the stairs.

Gurdi kicked a burning log and sparks leaped into the sky. "My simple life has been made full tonight. My friends, my many friends." He held his arms wide and spun around until he tumbled to the ground, where he squatted facing the fire. He clasped his hands and closed his eyes, squeezing tears from between the lashes.

We gathered around him. Kopries skipped and pointed at his dancing feet. "The mercy of God is seen in me," he murmured.

I watched the coals while they glowed and popped in the night air. "And in me, Kopries," I said. "I'm healed from my crippled spirit."

He put his arms around me and Gurdi hugged my legs.

Mother took my hand and kissed it. Her eyes sparkled, reflecting the embers. "Your faith is complete, my son. Jesus is the fulfillment of everything the prophets foretold, just as Paul and Barnabas said the first day they came to our little farm. We were so stubborn in our unbelief."

"We have so much to learn." I hugged her and she put her arms around me, resting her head on my chest.

"Together, Timothy, as we've always done."

Paul raised his hands, "Friends of Jesus, hear my prayer, Blessed be the God and Father of our Lord, our Messiah. Blessed be he who gave his Son who died, was buried, and rose again the third day. This is the good news.

"Here we have bread and wine left from our meal." Paul continued. "There is a way we celebrate our master that we must show you. Before he was betrayed on that fateful night, Jesus broke bread with his disciples, just as I'll do with you." Paul broke a loaf and passed it to Barnabas who took a piece and passed it on.

"The master himself served the bread that night," Paul said. "His very words were: 'This is my body, broken for you. Remember me in this way.'"

Then Paul ate the bread, looking up to the canopy of stars. We followed his example.

He did the same with the wine. Before passing it among us, he said, "Remember that Messiah was wounded and crucified. His shed blood made us right with God.

"Your belief in Messiah is fulfilled tonight. You believe, but without knowledge. Learn from me, as I have learned from our master."

Gurdi said, "I feel different. I don't understand the bread, the wine. Teach us more. Teach us here, tomorrow night."

"Eunice, with your permission?" asked Paul.

"Yes, of course. As my husband said, meet whenever you wish here."

"Then so be it, Gurdi. Come tomorrow. Bring food. We can't expect Andreas to supply our needs every day."

Paul and Barnabas stayed and taught until the summer heat baked the earth and turned the field straw yellow. On their last day, Father, Mother and I walked with them, in a refreshing light rain, to the Via Sebaste.

"We'll travel back the way we came," Barnabas said, "to appoint leaders in Iconium, Antioch and Salamis. Then we cross the Great Sea to Syria, our home. Pray that God will lead us back this way some day."

They marched away into the rain on the wide Roman road.

I felt abandoned and alone.

That winter, Father and I took his newly finished chest to Derbe. Even the risks of winter travel didn't stop him. He couldn't wait to show off his handiwork to the purchaser. Coming back, we were delayed by a snowstorm so fierce we couldn't see the road in front of us. We sheltered under our wagon, wore all our clothes and pulled over us the large cloth we'd used to cover the chest. When the storm subsided, snow banks had covered the curbstones. The road itself was nearly clear and we made our way home safely, though a day later than expected.

But the same storm caused more distress for Gurdi.

He told me had been delivering several large amphorae to a wine merchant. They were stacked on his little cart and he struggled to keep them balanced as he made his way through the snow-filled streets. He wrenched the cart about and picked his way between the crowds. He hummed to himself as he approached the wine shop and peered past the amphorae so he could guide the cart safely through the door. Just a few steps away, his load came to a sudden stop. The cart tipped forward and the load spilled onto the cobbled roadway and crashed against the shop walls. Gurdi tumbled to the trampled, dirty snow as people jumped out of the way and yelled at him.

"You stupid dwarf!" shouted one.

"You ignorant Lycaonian slave! Go back to your hole in the hills where you belong and take your useless cart with you," cried another.

"Sorry, master. So sorry," stammered Gurdi.

"Clean this mess up or I'll report you to the magistrate. Get to it!"

"Yes master." Gurdi stood up, too quickly, and lost his footing in the snow. He fell hard on his right arm. By the time he'd righted his cart, most of the people had continued on their way, but near the shop, Jonas sneered and gripped his cane. He raised his stick to strike but found it broken near the bottom so he turned it around and beat Gurdi with the knotted end.

"May God strike you without mercy," he hissed. "You're not wanted here and it's time you left. Your lies corrupt my people. Get out! Get out!"

Gurdi ducked beneath the stick. He turned his left shoulder to take the blows.

"Enough! That's enough, Jonas." Makis, the wine merchant waved Jonas off with his short beefy arm. "He's well beaten for the harm he's done. Be on your way so the wretch can clean up this mess."

Jonas lifted his head, his thin goatee pointed at Gurdi. Mumbling gibberish, he turned away and skulked off down the street.

Makis turned to Gurdi and spit through his teeth. "This will cost you, Gurdy. I paid for those amphorae and I expect you to cover my losses."

"Yes, of course. I am sorry Makis. I will pay. I will clean this up and will come with money tomorrow."

"You'll clean this up and pay me today or I'll have you arrested do you understand? Now get to work."

Gurdi quickly unloaded the undamaged amphorae and took them into the shop, then returned to his cart to clean up the shards. He was nearly finished when he noticed a wooden stick in the snow. He picked it up and saw that it was the broken end of Jonas' cane. He must have stuck his cane in the spokes of the cart's front wheel. Gurdi's heart sank. He could take beatings and insults for his mistakes, all his life he had done so. But this time, it wasn't his fault. It was pure, malicious hatred.

Gurdi had tried, every time he saw Jonas, to be polite and respectful. Was this how he was repaid? Sorrow drained him of life and left him hollow. He forgot his physical bruises, he told me, but his spirit wept over Jonas' contempt. As he picked his way back to Heracles' pottery studio, he saw the snow and remembered the psalm Paul had taught us:

"People hate him and refuse him,
Yet he carries our deepest pains and suffers our sorrows.
Cleanse me and I shall be whiter than snow."

Overwhelmed by the bruises suffered by his savior, and overcome by his failures, Gurdi fell to his knees in the snow, raised his hands to heaven and sang out his grief.

5

Revenge

In the early spring, two years after Paul and Barnabas had left us, Jonas struck his final blow.

It had snowed that day and traces of it littered the roadside and the shadows. Mother and I were at the south gate. Gurdi and Heracles had brought supplies and were helping us give food and drink to the hungry and penniless within the city walls.

I stood to stretch my back and wrapped my heavy cloak tightly around my tunic. The city had fallen quiet except for the crackling of warming fires the men had built. They squatted under threadbare blankets and stretched their palms toward the dancing flames. Heracles pointed toward the city wall at a bundle of rags covered in snow.

"Here's one we haven't seen before." He coughed. "Do we have any food left?"

"Yes, there's enough for one more," I answered.

As I reached into the bag, Heracles called out. "Mother Eunice, come quickly. This one needs you."

Mother stood slowly, straightening her back before plodding toward Heracles. These past two winters had aged her, but she never missed our nightly service to the poor. She smiled at Heracles and the wrinkles around her eyes signaled renewed energy and compassion. When she lovingly folded the hapless creature's shawl back to reveal the face, she recoiled and bit her knuckles. Her eyes tightened and closed, as she shook her head. I rushed to her side and put my arms around her. Peering from the motionless heap on the ground was the bloodied, swollen face of our dear friend, Rachel.

"No!" Mother screamed. "Not beloved Rachel. Dear God, what have they done to you?"

She held Rachel's face in her hands and kissed her wounds. She caressed her head and supported it like a newborn's.

Heracles offered wine and bread. Mother pushed them away. She bent her cheek close to Rachel's mouth. "She's alive. Her breaths are weak and slow."

Gurdi brought his wagon close. "My wagon, Mother. Can we move her?"

"I don't know, Gurdi, but bless you. Help me turn her. Gently now. There may be broken bones."

Rachel moaned deeply.

Mother felt every limb and ran her hands gently along her spine. "Bones may be broken. Deep bruises on her arms and face. Bleeding inside? I pray not. We must get her to the farm. I'll bathe and warm her. Pray she survives. All of you ... pray."

We took care to move evenly along the deeply-worn road. Every stone jarred the wagon and disturbed its wounded load. Even at the worst of the bumps, I heard no cry or moan. Rachel's silence alarmed me. Was she alive or dead?"

We reached the farm and Mother called out, "Timothy, build a fire in the oven. Heracles, Find Grandmother! Gather blankets and clean water."

Mother washed Rachel's face and hands. Gently she cleaned Rachel's wounds, bound up those that were bleeding and finally bundled her in blankets and lay her on a lambskin near the oven.

"Master, give her strength," she prayed.

Mother and Grandmother stayed in the *culina* where they kept the fire burning and cared for Rachel. I gathered wood and stacked it by the oven. "Go, Timothy," Mother said. "Lois and I will care for her."

The next morning, Mother told us that Rachel had taken a little water, poured carefully between her lips, but showed no change. Father was unusually quiet as we worked at the carpentry, and I thought about Rachel all day. We spent our evening meal mostly in silence, except for the sad report that Rachel hadn't improved.

On the third day, she opened her eyes and ate a little softened bread. By the end of the day she recognized Mother.

As Father and I walked home from the carpentry the next day, he put his arm on my shoulder. "Will Rachel get better, Timothy? What does your god tell you?"

"I hear no response from Jesus when I pray. Only a dark silence."

"Someone must pay, Timothy."

"Her family rejected her, Father. There's no one to plead her case. If it's a matter of Jewish law, we have no standing. If Roman, they'll turn their backs against us, as they always do."

The journey home seemed longer that day.

Rachel awoke at first light the following morning and begged for food and drink. Mother propped her up against the *culina* wall and gave her bread, cheese, and water, then called us. Rachel's bruises were darker than the day we'd found her and one eye was nearly closed from swelling. A deep slash on her cheek wept fluid and Mother blotted it with cotton.

"It needs air to heal," she explained.

She swept Rachel's hair back, away from her face. "Take your time, dear. Tell us everything."

Rachel sipped some water. She tried to smile, but her mouth twisted in a lopsided grimace. She whispered through cracked lips, "I should have expected it. Prepared myself. My fault." She took another drink of water.

Father, Grandmother, and I sat close by on the kitchen stools so we could hear.

"I knew Amram would lose his temper if he caught me

worshipping Jesus," Rachel whispered. "My little shrine. Kept hidden. A small cross. Two branches tied in the center, to remind me of his suffering. After he left the house, I unwrapped it from its cotton cover."

She closed her eyes and her lips narrowed into a weak smile. She forced herself to take a breath. Her brow tightened and she shuddered as she continued. "Amram burst through the door."

Tears moistened her lashes. "He startled me. Couldn't move. 'Too cold,' he called. 'I need my cloak.' Father was behind him. Saw me on my knees before my cross."

Her hands began to shake and Mother quickly took the cup from her. She coughed and held her ribs before continuing.

"Father screamed, 'Blasphemer! Idol worshipper! Accursed symbol of Roman torture. You insult our holy God. Desecrate our family's name.' He pushed me down and beat me with his stick. He shouted, 'Shamed me, Rachel. You are no daughter of mine.'"

She put her head on Mother's shoulder and sobbed. Mother gently stroked Rachel's back. "Shh, shh. You're safe here. We'll care for you."

Rachel wiped her tears with the back of her hand. "There's more," she said.

"Amram threw me into the street. People gathered. 'You've disgraced my good name,' he declared. 'I divorce you. Before witnesses.' And again he said it, to fulfill the law." Her shoulders throbbed and she gasped for breath. We waited until she could speak again.

"I lay in the dust. They tore stones from the curb. I tried to crawl away. Father and husband hurled rocks at me. Blackness covered me until I awoke here."

Rachel was outcast, disowned by her family and the Judean community. Grandmother slipped quietly from her chair and sat at Rachel's feet, stroking her legs. "My poor dear," she cried.

Father pulled at his beard. His hands curled into tight fists. His anger was as strong as Grandmother's compassion. "Your own father," he spat, through clenched teeth. "And your husband. The ones you trust to protect you. Wicked men. Wicked, wicked men." He turned and left the *culina*.

I gritted my teeth against my own anger. I knew men could be cruel and that some beat their wives and even their daughters, but this was the first time I saw, up close, the horrible wounds caused by such brutality. Rachel's beauty was marred forever and her spirit broken. I wanted to unleash my anger against Jonas and Amram.

Mother put her arms around Rachel. "Stay with us. Be my daughter in faith. Like Naomi was to Ruth. Where I go, you'll go. Where I stay, you'll stay. My people will be your people and my God is your God."

She rocked Rachel in her arms and sang songs I knew from childhood. Soon, Rachel surrendered to sleep's healing balm.

I slipped out, full of anger. I wanted to avenge the beating. As I crossed the courtyard, Gurdi pushed his wagon through our gate.

"Timothy. My friend. I've come. Come to see Rachel. I have wine and nuts, olives and cheese. She needs to get strong. I bring food and drink."

I kicked up a swirl of dust. I glared at him as if he were a stranger. My jaw tightened. I hissed like a wild animal.

Gurdi stepped back. "My friend, calm yourself. What is it?"

I dropped my hands and shook my head. "Rachel is not the woman she was. She's scarred outside and battered inside. What can I do, Gurdi? I hate Jonas and Amram."

Father strode from the tool shed with an axe in his hand and an old sword, freshly sharpened, strapped to his waist. "Come, Timothy. We'll set this right."

He strode past Gurdi then turned back. "Wait here, little one. Help the women care for Rachel." He thrust the axe into my hand and stepped toward the gate. The axe felt powerful. I yearned to slice scars in the persecutors' faces.

Gurdi, small though he was, pushed his cart in our way and held up his hand. He stood with his feet planted and his eyes wide. His voice came lower, more forcefully than I'd ever heard. "You are like them. Angry men. Blind. Timothy, you follow Jesus in rage?"

He glared at me, then at Father. "Andreas, you taught your son to be calm. Wise words win wars. Wars of the tongue. Now you wear your weapon?"

Father raised his brows and took his hand from his sword. The axe suddenly felt too heavy in my grip. I stared at its keen steel edge. I saw my face reflected by the red morning sun, as if bathed in blood. The blade fell from my fingers and thudded to the dirt.

Gurdi slowly drew Father's sword from its sheath and dropped it beside the axe. "Come, let's sit. Eat. You have wounds to heal. Rage must go and calm return."

He took Father's arm and led us to the *excedra* below Grandmother's room. "You can't follow Jesus in anger, my friends. You must learn his peace."

Father shook his head and twisted his mouth. He looked as confused as I felt.

Gurdi held his hands in front of him as if opening a scroll. "Begin with truth. To those who would stone the unfaithful woman, our master said, 'Let he who has no sin cast the first stone.' Jonas had no right. Amram had no right. That is truth."

Though I felt anger rising again, Gurdi's dark-eyed gaze stopped me. "And you have no right to strike others out of hatred," he said.

Father studied the ground in front of him and scratched his cheek.

Gurdi motioned for us to sit on the stairs. Now we were eye to eye.

"Add to truth, goodness. Your wise man said, 'When a man's ways please the Lord, he makes even his enemies to be at peace with him.' Paul taught me this."

"And Mother taught me, Gurdi," I said.

Father nodded. "I know the teaching. Eunice has said it often. You're right to remind us, Gurdi. I'm ashamed. But tell us how to bring justice against Rachel's father and husband."

Gurdi waved his hand back and forth. "Not for you, my friends. Not for you. Justice is Jehovah's, not yours."

Father stood. "What then? We do nothing?"

"If your enemy is hungry, give him food to eat. If he is thirsty, give him water to drink. Truth, goodness, love. That is Messiah's way."

"They'll laugh at us. The whole city will laugh us to scorn." Father marched to where our weapons lay in the dust. "I'll put these away, my little friend, but your pearls of wisdom don't persuade me. There's another way and I'll find it."

Gurdi stood and gripped my arm. "Don't follow him, Timothy. You must teach your father. He will see Messiah's truth if you hold to the teaching. Do good to your enemies."

I wasted no time testing Gurdi's advice. The next day, Mother packed a basket of food and drink and I took it with me to Lystra. As soon as we opened the carpentry, I rushed across the town square to the metalsmiths, Hiram and Jotham. Though they worshipped at the river with Jonas, they hadn't stopped doing business with us despite Rabbi Shemuel's decree. I found Hiram behind his shop pounding a slug of iron into a spike. He wore only a light tunic under a leather apron.

He looked at my thick coat. "You won't need that here, my boy. My forge defeats the most frigid cold." He threw the nail into a bucket and whipped another slug onto the anvil. "What's that?" He dropped his tongs and peeked into the basket. "Ahh food and drink. Early, but I'll eat any time. A man works up an appetite in this heat." He reached out his massive paw.

I pulled the basket away. "No, my friend. Not for you and you'll never guess whose stomach it'll fill."

"Must be them beggars at the city gate. You've a soft spot for them." He eyed the food greedily.

I broke a chunk off the loaf. "Here. A bribe. I want you to do something for me."

Hiram scooped the bread out of my hand and into his massive mouth before I could take a breath. "What?" he mumbled.

"Give this to Jonas." I put the basket on his workbench.

Hiram turned back to his anvil. "You're dull in the head." He wiped the sweat from his broad forehead and lifted his tongs. "You're as simple as this plug of iron. The man hates you. He won't take it."

"Don't tell him who it's from. And I'll bring another every day until Sabbath. After today, leave it on his doorstep. Will you do it?"

"I will, but you're mad," he said.

Five days later, on Sabbath, I dressed in my fringed tunic and wore my prayer shawl for the holy day. I took the food basket to Jonas myself. I put it on his doorstep and stood next to it until he came out to go to morning prayers.

The door opened and an ashen, bony arm reached out to grasp the basket's handle.

I stepped closer. "Shalom, Jonas."

"Shalom," he said, and looked up to see who it was.

His hair was greyer than I remembered and his face colourless, like a clouded winter sky. He made no sign that he recognized me, so I dropped my shawl away from my face. "It's Timothy, son of Andreas," I said. "Do you have enough food?"

"Timothy? Andreas?" His eyes widened and he raised his walking stick as he'd done years before when he'd tried to strike me with it.

"Rachel!" he cried. He swung his stick at me and fell back against the doorpost. I held his arm to stop him tumbling to the ground and gently lowered him to the step. He coughed and choked as he tried to speak.

"Let me help." I took the flagon of wine from the basket and held it to his mouth. He swallowed and licked his lips. He stared at me then tried to pull himself back into his house like a hare scurrying from a fox.

"You! You stole my daughter, ruined my life. Get away!"

"No," I said in an even tone. "You beat your daughter and threw her out. You banished the light of her devotion to keep the darkness of your tradition. But you can't conquer her love. Or ours." I pushed the basket through his doorway.

He stumbled to his feet and stiffened his back. He glared and shook his stick, then opened his mouth and formed words, but only coughed weakly. He clutched his chest and hobbled back, throwing the door shut behind him. I heard the bolt slide into its hasp.

I turned and walked through the narrow streets and pulled my shawl over my head. I crossed the market square. "May the Lord bless you and keep you," I prayed. "May he cause his Spirit to shine on you and be gracious to you. May he lift up his smile on you and give you peace."

Rachel never fully recovered from her wounds. The scars on her face gradually faded and some of her former beauty shone through, but she suffered pain in her hip and right knee. She walked with a limp for the rest of her life. Her wounds were a constant reminder that the love of Jesus might be met, not with gratitude, but with rage.

I saw Jonas one day through the carpentry door. He was standing at a market stall, testing the ripeness of some vegetables. He looked noticeably older and frail. He leaned more heavily on his stick, and when he moved on, it was with a plodding, spiritless gait. I felt sorry for him and wondered who had suffered the greater loss, he or Rachel.

Father came to my side, rested his heavy hand on my shoulder and lifted one calloused finger toward Jonas. "He's a beaten man."

"No, Father, Rachel was beaten, and that old man is responsible. He's been against us from the start and no kindness changes that."

He pulled at his graying beard. "True. I've heard that losing Rachel has broken him. He has no strength left. Jotham thinks he wants to die and leave his misery behind. I doubt you'll have more trouble from him."

He kicked at a broken amphora. "He's like baked clay. His creeds can no longer be moulded. He chose to fight and it's ruined him. You know, the Greeks and Romans accept all gods as long as they don't threaten the empire. Preach to them, my son. Leave these self-righteous ones alone."

A harshness entered his voice. "They'll fight you over this."

"They have a right to know the truth. I can't ignore them."

"The truth, Timothy!" He slapped his leather apron. "There are many truths. If you insist on only one, there'll be trouble."

I held up my hand. "I believe what I believe. I can't change what truth is for me. I hope you can see it yourself one day."

6

Called

A FEW WEEKS AFTER RACHEL WAS BEATEN, GURDI CALLED ALL FOLLOWERS of the Nazarene to hear from a teacher from Derbe, a young carpenter, named Gaius. I knew him from the games competition. He was shorter and older than me, with a stocky build and close-cut curly black hair. During the two years since Paul and Barnabas had left, Gaius had come several times to help us learn more about Jesus.

It was a cold evening in early spring when we met in our home's open courtyard. Gurdi stood on a milking bench and Kopries stood beside him. Even though Gaius hadn't arrived, Gurdi called out for silence so we could begin. His voice was smothered by excited shouts in the crowd. "Paul has returned."

I stretched to see over the people, but only saw the crowd shift as they moved aside for the visitors. Then I saw a tall stranger behind Gaius, but my eyes locked on the short, bandy-legged, goateed man at his side.

"Paul!" I shouted, and ran to him. "We didn't know you were coming." I pulled him into a great hug. My mouth stretched into a smile as wide as the Aegean. I'd hoped Paul would return. I needed more teaching.

"Timothy, my friend and disciple." He held me at arm's length.

"You've become a man, tall and strong. Where's the boy I left behind?"

"Ah, he's lurking in here," I said, touching my heart. "Sometimes he takes control, though he's not the same. But look at you. I see the grey creeping into the dark hair over your ears, a few more lines on your face. Dignity to match the wisdom of a great teacher"

"If so, it's Jehovah's wisdom, not my own."

Paul turned to the people. "There's such a crowd. Are they all believers?"

"Yes Paul! And we've told them everything about you. They must hear your words of truth. Please teach us tonight. Will you?"

"I will, my friend." He laughed.

Paul turned and grasped Gurdi's arm, then reached out to Kopries and embraced him. "Your numbers have grown. Silas, come and meet these church leaders."

A tall, powerfully-built man with a full beard and a head of wavy black hair strode from the crowd and stood beside Paul.

"God love you," he said, in a strong, deep voice. "Paul talked about you all the way from Tarsus. The way he boasted, I expected to meet a crowd of giants. Surely, you're giants in faith."

"Silas is from Jerusalem," Paul said, "and you know Gaius. My faithful companions on our long journey."

He looked past the crowd at Mother standing in the culina doorway.

When Mother saw Paul, she smiled the way she did on Sabbath when I'd take my place at the head of the table.

"One moment before I begin," Paul said. He left the crowd and walked to the culina.

He held his hands together in front of him and bowed his head. "Eunice, blessed mother to all these followers of Messiah. I was told in Syria of the foundation you've laid for the gospel. Bless you. Now, rest from your service and hear the master's words as he taught me and as I heard from his first disciples. Come."

Mother followed Paul to the center of the courtyard. He placed her at the front where she could hear well, then turned and clapped his hands.

"Good Christians of Lystra. I am Paul. As a young man in Jerusalem, the city of peace, I studied under Gamaliel, the great teacher of the law and prophets. Later I learned from those who followed the Nazarene. Today I bring the words of Jesus, Messiah."

The name fluttered like a butterfly from mouth to ear as its holiness settled among us. I pulled my hands to my chest and closed my eyes. The words of the Nazarene, at last.

Slowly, I sank to the ground and sat with my eyes fixed on the only man I knew who'd been with those who lived with Jesus. Soon everyone sat on the cold ground to see Paul better.

"His name is Jesus, Christos." Paul pointed to the heavens. "Jehovah anointed him as Savior. Jesus said, 'I am the Son of God.'"

Kopries whispered, "Then God healed me." He held his hands to his face and nodded his head. "God healed me."

"Yes, Kopries, God healed you. He healed, raised the dead and was raised from death himself. Yet he suffered the death of a common criminal."

Paul showed that our ancient scriptures were fulfilled in Jesus. I was determined to learn as much as I could from him and listened intently until the night became icy. We pulled our cloaks around us and stomped our feet to keep them from freezing.

"I see it's getting late, and cold," Paul said. "More another day."

Most people left quickly to get home and build a fire. Kopries and Gurdi stayed, along with our new guests. Mother ushered us to the culina, the warmest place, full of the aroma of fresh bread. Rachel and Grandmother had heated some watered wine with honey to go with the bread and there was some cheese.

"Grandmother Lois," Paul said, and gently hugged her. "Once again, you serve me in this home. Bless you. And who's this young lady?" Rachel was turned away from us with her shawl pulled over her head and face.

"This is Rachel," Grandmother said. "She was beaten for her faith and lives with us now."

"My, my, Rachel. Don't be afraid, my dear," Paul said. "You have battle scars of a soldier of the cross. You'll be honoured in heaven for your courage and spiritual beauty. Christ's splendour will cover all your wounds."

Rachel turned toward us and slowly folded back her shawl.

I gasped. The scars had given her face strength and tenderness.

"Rachel, you are beautiful," said Gurdi. "Do you know? See, Kopries. See, Timothy. Rachel is beautiful. God has turned your suffering into beauty. Surely, we see a miracle this night. Is it not so, Paul?"

"It's true, Gurdi. God bless you, Rachel. Stay with us, please, and hear my instructions to these leaders of Lystra."

Rachel smiled at Paul's kindness. "Thank you, Paul. You bring joy to my heart." She brought a platter of bread and cheese. Her face stayed uncovered and she held her head proudly as she served.

Paul broke the bread and passed it around. "How do you worship?" he asked. Do you honour Sabbath? Do you celebrate Passover? In some churches, arguments have broken out about the old Judean customs."

He pointed at me. "What about here in Lystra, Timothy?"

I drank some wine. Its warmth flowed through me and cleared my throat. "Rabbi Shemuel has banned us from worship at the river. Most of the new believers don't know our ancient practices. We meet on the first day of the week to celebrate Jesus' resurrection. Here at home, our family celebrates Sabbath and Passover. Are we wrong to do this?"

"No, my son. I met with Christian leaders in Jerusalem. I'm to tell you not to let your worship divide you. Don't make anyone take up Judean practices foreign to them. Keep to the central teachings of Jesus. It's good you've found a way to worship together."

Paul finished his wine. He gave the goblet to Mother and thanked her. He stood slowly and yawned. "Now, it's late and we've traveled all day. It's time to rest."

Mother asked me to take Paul, Silas and Gaius to their room next to mine and to make sure they had all they needed. I took one of their bags and we crossed the courtyard.

Paul took my arm. "Timothy, I'd like to talk with you tomorrow. Could we meet before you start work?"

"Of course, Paul. I help Mother with the livestock feeding at first light. Look for me in the stables or the chicken pen."

"I will. Sleep well, Timothy."

"Sleep well," I answered.

Barna, our yearling ewe, nudged my hand as I fed her fresh grain. I'd filled the troughs for the others, but always started her by hand. She was born the spring after Paul and Barnabas left Lystra and I'd missed them badly, so I gave her a name that would remind me to pray for them during the morning feeding. I worked by candlelight in the gray dawn. The flickering light cast shadows in the stalls and barely reached the rafters. I wondered why Paul wanted to meet with me, but the goat's soft braying and mewling and the smells of fur and straw bedding gave me a deep sense of calm. The world in the stable was at peace.

"I see you start early, Timothy," Paul said as he stepped over the doorsill. He wore a wool paenula over his tunic. His goatee glistened from an early wash.

"It's my routine," I answered. "If I'm not ready with their feed once the light breaks, they make a lot of noise."

Paul stepped around the milking stool and scooped some grain from the bin. He held it out to Barna and smiled as she lapped it from his hand. "I enjoy the morning stillness," he said. "Prayer is the best preparation for the day. I would have come earlier but for that. Can I help fill the feed bins?"

"Yes, of course. I'll milk the ewes. Then we'll have time for that talk you wanted. In fact, I'm counting on you. I told Mother I wouldn't need her help this morning."

We finished quickly, so I suggested we walk down to the stream for water while we talked. I took Barna with us and tethered her to the tree so she could graze on the lush grass.

"Word of your love for the poor and the hostility you've faced has spread far beyond the walls of Lystra, my friend," Paul said. "Your name is spoken of as a man of character and leadership."

"I do what's right as a follower of Jesus," I said.

We filled two ewers with water and Paul rested for a moment against a tree. The water flowed crystal clear along the narrow channel. Its course would take it to Lystra, then further south where others would quench their thirst from its faithful supply.

"I want you to come on our journey," Paul said. "Travel with us as we build up the churches and bring the gospel to new places. Gurdi and Kopries have established themselves as leaders here. They'll keep building the church. I believe God has something great in store for you. He can change the world through men who have surrendered to his way. Pray about this. I'll expect your answer within a day," he said.

He gripped my arm and smiled, then left me, dumbstruck, under the trees by the steam. Water flowed and leaves stirred in the wind but I was paralyzed, my feet frozen to the ground.

It seemed another life when Barnabas had told me it would be cowardly if I stayed home. I'd become so busy with God's work in Lystra that I'd forgotten Barnabas' words.

I watched the water bubbling by. A piece of bark floated lazily along. A tiny frog leaped from the shore and landed on the bark. The bark bobbled this way and that until the bushes along the bank hid it from view. Restlessness grew within me. I imagined a new life. I climbed the hill to the stables and retrieved the fresh milk. By the time I'd reached the *culina*, I'd decided I would join Paul.

I stepped gingerly into the room, where Father and Mother shared first bread. I wondered how I'd tell them. How would they manage without me?

"Sit, my child," Mother said. "Warm your bones and fill that cavernous mouth of yours. Ahh, milk." Mother took the jug and poured the frothy liquid into the butter churn.

Father was hunched over a cup of warmed honey-wine with raisins. He tore a piece of bread and shoved it into his mouth followed by a gulp of mead. Some spilled on his graying beard and he wiped his arm across his face.

"Eat up, Son. There's work to do. No time to waste." He groaned and pushed himself to his feet, then stretched and pushed his fist into his back. "I'll be in the tool shed."

"Wait. I have something to tell you."

Father turned from the doorway. "Be quick about it. Hiram and Jotham want us to start on their roof today. If we don't get support on the corners, it'll buckle and the weight of the mud and thatch will bring it down."

"I know. This won't take long."

Mother held out a cup and I drank the honey-wine, draining it. As I put it back in her hand she smiled up at me. "I see it in your eyes, today," she said. "You're a man. You have your father's strength, and there's firmness in your jaw. What have you decided?"

Father's eyebrows twisted and he cocked his head. "What are you saying, wife? Are you a seer? He's still the same lad."

I put my arm around Mother and faced Father. "She knows me well, Father." I took a deep breath. "It's time for me to leave, to make my own way. Paul wants me to go with him and a voice inside says I must."

Mother took my hand and held it tightly. She shut her eyes. Tears formed between the lids. She leaned her head against my shoulder.

Father threw his arms wide and embraced us. He smiled. Spider-leg wrinkles creased around his eyes. "It's about time you earned your living, Timothy," he teased.

Mother couldn't be so lighthearted. "Timothy, Paul's given you a great honour. I can't possibly refuse if it's your desire, but how will we cope on the farm and in Andreas' shop? We need you."

"I know, Mother. That's my one concern," I said.

"We'll manage," said Father. "Rachel will keep helping on the farm in return for her bed and I'll hire and train a carpenter. One of your young Christians might brave my rough ways and ill humor. Each one you rescue from the street needs a living. No one can replace my son, but there's a job here for the right man."

"Thank you Father. Does that mean I can go with Paul?"

"Truth is, Timothy, you can go no matter what we say, but we're proud that you ask. We'll miss you, son, but I'm sure you'll be back some day."

"Paul hasn't said, Father. I'm sorry. I was so intent on going, I didn't even think about returning."

Mother's eyes were wet with tears. "You must, Timothy. It would break my heart not to see you again."

"Then we'll have faith in the master for my return. He wouldn't wish your heart broken. We must trust him, Mother."

I told Father I'd get help for the day's work and meet him at Hiram's. Then I went in search of Gaius to tell him I'd be travelling with them. I found him leaning against the oak tree where I'd tethered our goat that morning. He was reading a scroll and was so intent on it he didn't realize that the goat's rope was winding around his feet. If he moved quickly, he'd surely fall. I kept out of sight and crept near, then pulled the rope just hard enough to lift his feet and send him to the ground.

"Ah, asleep on the job, Gaius. I caught you," I said.

"Whoa, Timothy!" Gaius eyes widened and a smile began to play on his lips. "You rascal. What are you up to?"

"You made it easy," I said. "Deep in study. What's stealing your attention?"

I sat down beside him.

"Paul's teachings. He taught this one night: 'Watch out! Know what's happening around you. Don't waste your life. Make the most of every opportunity and understand what the master wants you to do.' He said it's the definition of a prophet."

"I thought a prophet told the future."

"Paul says a prophet is someone who can tell you God's will for now or for the future," said Gaius.

"Then I'm a prophet," I said. "I can tell you God's will for today and for some time into the future."

"Well don't keep me in suspense, Timothy."

"Paul asked if I'd travel with him and I'm going to say yes. We'll be journeying together, Gaius. That's God's will," I said.

"Wonderful, Timothy, but I'm not going on with Paul. When he's finished in Lystra, I'm returning to Derbe."

There was no disappointment in his rugged face, just calm acceptance.

"You're going back? I thought you were with him on this mission."

"No, not now. He asked me, but I'm not ready. I'm hoping to join him in a year or so. But it's right that you go. Now's your time. I told Paul about you and urged him to add you to his team. I've been praying that you'd accept because I believe God has prepared you for this."

"Well, I hope you're right. In the meantime, get on your feet. Father needs me at the shop and we could use your help. We'll go to Lystra, do the work and get back before dark. Will you come?" I asked.

"Absolutely, and I'm going to beat you there, even if you run like a deer."

7

Still Small Voice

THE NEXT MORNING ON THE WAY TO LYSTRA, PAUL AND I WALKED together behind Father, Gaius, and Silas.

"Paul," I said. "I've decided to come with you."

He walked with his head down and his hands behind his back. Then he looked at me with his small black eyes.

"Wonderful, Timothy. Now, I have a more difficult request. If you join us, you must be circumcised."

Old Jonas' words echoed in my head. 'You must be circumcised.' Anger rose in me at the memory. How could I now be hearing this from the apostle who had told us we should not expect gentile Christians to follow Judean customs?

"Circumcised?" I croaked when I discovered my voice. "Why would you ask me to do this? I fought Jonas over it for two years."

"I'm sorry. I should have prepared you better. We take the gospel to the Judeans at their strict synagogues where the uncircumcised aren't allowed. I can't take you on the journey unless you're circumcised."

He shrugged and lifted his palms. "It's your decision, but the two are yoked like oxen. To join us, you must submit to this rite."

Normally I admired Paul's educated speech and tried to copy him, but now it sounded overbearing. I felt he was being pompous, inflexible and contradictory.

"I understand," I said, "but I don't agree. You say I must be circumcised to be acceptable to Jews. Jonas said the same thing and I refused. I can't change my mind now. It would be two-faced of me. I'm sorry. You'll have to go without me."

I turned away from Paul and hurried along the road.

I heard Paul's voice behind me. "Timothy, don't be so hasty."

His words were silenced by one question that pounded in my head. How can this be? Mother, Grandmother, Gaius, all had said I should go with Paul and now it was impossible. Though I walked in sunshine under a vast blue sky, I felt like I'd entered a dark tunnel. My future had become a lifetime in the carpentry shop. Until this hour, I'd loved Lystra, our farm, our carpentry. Now they were just dashed hopes.

I tried to keep my somber mood from Gaius as we worked on Hiram's roof. Father had left us alone to rough-hew supports for the new roof and I threw my anger into each cut against the strong cypress. When I stopped, the sun was high overhead. I wiped my brow, sat astride the board I was shaping and dropped my adze to the ground.

Gaius' stocky arms flexed and his muscled abdomen glistened as he chopped. He stopped and turned to me with a wide grin. Drops of sweat fell from his nose and chin until he wiped them away with his forearm. I smiled back at him and realized that my anger was gone. Only confusion remained.

"I can keep up with you, my friend," I said, "but not if we go on until dark. I need rest and shade."

Gaius brushed the dust and shavings from his torso. "And food," he said. "I've worked up a hunger." He stepped over the wood. "You've been quiet all morning, Timothy. You're brooding over something. Tell me before it rots your soul."

"I do need your advice. Bring the flask, I'll take the pouch. We'll sit by the well in the sycamore shade. My head is full of darkness."

Gaius scooped up the flask from the shade of the wall and we strode down the hill to the well. He put his arm on my shoulder. "Sounds ominous. Tell me all."

"I've told Paul I won't go with him."

He took the flask from his lips and held it toward me as he wiped his mouth.

"He told me I must be circumcised to join him," I said. "I can't."

Gaius took a loaf of bread, broke it and handed me half.

I held the bread, but spoke before taking a bite. "I was a Jew. Now I follow the Nazarene. I can't go back."

"And you can't go on. I understand." He waved his hand as if clearing shavings from a worktop. "I can't help, Timothy. I'm not Judean. We Greeks don't cut the flesh in ritual. Perhaps Silas? He's Judean and well taught. Ask him about Jesus' baptism. He told us it wasn't necessary, but the messiah did it anyway."

"Silas? I hardly know him." We sat in silence for a moment. Tightness gripped my chest. I didn't want to dismiss Gaius' suggestion, but I feared Silas would tell me the same as Paul. Finally I said, "I'll go to Gurdi. He has a simple wisdom, like Solomon's. I can trust him."

Gaius nodded and drained the last of the wine. He picked up the pouch and strode back to our workplace. Slowly I picked up the heavy adze. Its blade seemed dull the rest of the day. We worked late to get the corner posts in place and support them with cross pieces. As soon as the last brace was fastened, I handed Gaius my tools. "Would you take these to the shop and tell Mother that I'll be with Gurdi? Don't say anything about my decision. Promise me, friend." He took the adze and cocked his head at me. I knew he didn't like what I was asking him to do.

He lifted the tools over his hefty shoulder. "God guide you, Timothy." I clapped him on his arm and trotted south toward Gurdi's forest hideaway. If I kept up a good pace, I'd be there by dusk.

As I closed on Gurdi's hut, I called out. "Gurdi, it's Timothy." The door of rough branches that concealed his hut opened and Gurdi stood, almost invisible under the dappled moonlight. He smiled when he saw me, baring his crooked teeth. His familiar high cheekbones and low brows had become, to me, an icon of good sense.

"You are here. My friend. Come. Enter my home." He swung his knotted, black hair in a circle as he led the way. I bent low through the doorway and waited for my eyes to adjust to the darkness. I finally saw the dirt floor, stone table and gnarled wood stools. Gurdi poured wine into clay cups and set broken bread and cheese on the table. "Eat, Timothy. It's late. You must eat."

I took some bread and dipped it into the wine to soften it. After my long run, I drank and ate greedily. Thoughts ran about in my head like ants near a nest. I couldn't snatch a word or question to tell my friend what troubled me. Finally, I wiped my mouth and sat back on the stool.

"I'm trapped, Gurdi. I'm lost in a deep pit and can't see the light." I covered my head with my hands.

"Do not think. Do not chase troubles in your head. Seek peace. Be calm." Gurdi gently placed my hands on the table and covered my head with his own strong, calloused hands. I felt their warmth and slowly, my mind settled while his quiet voice relaxed me. "Remember, Jehovah is your shepherd. He chooses green pastures, still waters for rest."

I pictured black clouds drifting away. Then the sun brightened a grassy meadow by a small lake. A goose glided onto the water and left a trail behind that was gently absorbed into the calm surface. She curved her neck gracefully and picked at her wing feathers. My muscles relaxed. I felt calm.

"Better," Gurdi said. "The words will come now, I think." He dropped his hands and pulled his stool to my side. He looked into my eyes and waited.

I turned my palms up on the table. "I've been betrayed by the man I trusted the most."

"Jesus was betrayed," Gurdi whispered. "You feel his suffering."

"I've lost myself. I don't know who I am or what I must do."

"What does the master call you to do? That is what matters. Seek his voice and live."

Slowly, I looked at Gurdi. He pressed his lips together and smiled. I knew what Paul wanted me to do. That was the source of my distress.

"But Paul?" I began.

Gurdi held both hands up. "The master. Jesus, not Paul. Paul is a follower. Disciple, not master. You listen to the wrong voice."

The wrong voice. It was Jesus' voice I must obey, not Paul's. When they agree, allegiance is clear. If they differ, I must hear Jesus' words only.

"Gurdi, you speak with wisdom. I need to go. I'll wait in the stable for the voice of the Nazarene."

"It's dark. Late. You cannot find your way."

"No, there's a full moon. I'll find my way."

The moon's silvery glow made the road back to Lystra easy to follow. I crept silently into our farmyard, stepped into the stable and climbed into Barna's stall. She butted against my leg. "Shhh," I whispered. "Sleep, little one. I need your warmth tonight." I huddled on the straw beside her and waited for her to settle. I lay back on her soft, shaggy wool and rested as my breathing slowed.

The stable had become my private place in the dark hours. The familiar smell of dry straw and warm animals comforted me. Only a slight stirring broke the silence, probably a mouse scurrying through the straw bedding. Then an owl's distant hooting.

"Come, Jesus," I whispered. "Speak to me."

The night wrapped its dark arms around me. I felt safe and warm. I may have slept a little. At some point, I felt the presence of another nearby. "Barna," I thought in my grogginess.

Was I dreaming when I heard the words that came softly to my ear? *My child, take comfort in my presence.*

I sat up and peered toward the voice. It must be Jesus. "Messiah?" I reached toward the sound, but my hand grasped only cool air.

There's nothing you can touch. I am wind. You are substance, with strength to bring life to the dead, or comfort to the bereaved.

"No, master, not me, though I'd hoped to learn from your apostle."

A draft rippled along my cloak. I shivered.

You've taken a stand against Jonas. His heart has turned to stone and you cling to your defiance as a point of pride.

I waited in the still silence until I couldn't bear it. "Yes," I muttered. "I thought it would be false to do otherwise."

A noise disturbed the stall. Goats stirring, maybe.

And now you take a stand against Paul's request.

"Is that wrong? He said there's no merit in it."

The voice became stern. *Are you so determined not to go to my people in their synagogues? A fox trapped in a rock-fall would chew off its paw to gain release. Yet you won't lose a scrap of flesh so you might bring freedom to people imprisoned in their creed.*

Selfish, I thought, and stubborn. Childish.

It's not you alone I love. All who tread this earth, slake their thirst from heaven's rain and dine on my garden's food are precious to me. Dear lamb, my loving presence is with you forever.

"Forever," I thought. Messiah longed for even Jonas and Shemuel to enjoy his loving presence, and others in synagogues all over Galatia. Forever is a long, long time.

I fell asleep with those thoughts.

When I awoke, the darkness had turned from coal black to ash. The rooster crowed, almost drowning out Jesus' last words: *Many have no love like mine.*

I stared at the grey outline of the stalls. A growing brightness struggled through the spaces between the boards. I felt as if someone I loved had died and left me.

I rubbed my eyes and Barna lifted her head. She sat on her haunches and butted my leg.

"All right, my hungry ewe."

I filled all the bins and fetched water.

It was Sabbath morning. The Judeans would be meeting for worship at the tent by the river. Although I'd been banished, Silas was unknown, a traveller from Jerusalem. He would be welcome. Would Jonas and the rabbi accept me if I were with Silas?

I hurried across the yard. Silas' place was empty and I moved silently to avoid meeting Father or Mother. I would talk to them later. I washed and pulled on my fringed tunic. I carried my *tallith*, unsure if an outcast was allowed to wear the prayer shawl. I rushed along the road to catch up to Silas.

Just as I came to Lystra, Rabbi Shemuel in his white robes and ornate headpiece strode through the gates. Amram, Rachel's divorced husband, and Jonas were right behind him. The rabbi saw me and the shawl I carried in my arms. I hastily pulled it over my head, but it was too late.

Shemuel threw both arms in the air and stepped back as if I were a putrid carcass.

"Away from me!" he screamed. "Abomination! You wear the raiment of the faith but believe the lie. Uncircumcised infidel! Your body carries the sign of unbelief."

He swept up his robes and gestured to his followers. "Get him away from me. I can't look on his deceit."

Amram rushed at me, waddling on pudgy legs. He snatched the *tallith* from my head. I staggered back and fell hard to the river trail. A stabbing pain shot through my ankle.

He threw my shawl at my face and twisted his fat cheeks into a snarl, "You're worse than the swine that vomit filthy worms!" He turned and the three of them crossed the street to pass me by, then crossed back to reach the path to their holy tent.

The mere sight of me now repelled the men who once accepted me, son of a Hebrew woman, into their place of worship. "Lord, what have I become?" I whispered.

Circumcision would never restore their trust in me, but it might prevent synagogues in other cities from seeing me as Shemuel did.

Paul was right. I had to be circumcised.

8

Darkness

I ROLLED ONTO MY SIDE AND RUBBED MY ANKLE. IT WAS SWOLLEN AND blue. I pushed myself to a kneeling position then stood. With most of my weight on the good foot, I was able to hobble a few steps to the city wall where I leaned for support. A tall man in Judean dress, with a full beard and strong features strode by and on to the river path without seeing me. It was Silas.

"Silas, Help!" I called.

He rushed over and took my arm. "Timothy. What happened?"

"I've wrenched my ankle. I need help to get home."

Silas put his shoulder under mine, taking the weight off my foot. "Let's try this. If it's too far, I'll fetch a cart from Heracles. You'll look particularly fine perched there on Sabbath morning." He laughed and helped me limp along the road.

"I'm sorry," I said. "You'll miss the worship. I was on my way there. I wanted to talk with you, but the rabbi waylaid me."

"The rabbi? What happened?"

"He's banished all Christ followers from the tent of worship, Silas. He'll do the same with you when he discovers your allegiance. When he saw me wearing the tallith, he was outraged." I pointed to my foot. "This is the result."

"I see," Silas said. "I had hoped to worship with my countrymen once, at least, before being discovered. If they listened to the Nazarene's teachings, they'd find peace to heal their anger."

We reached a *stade* marker by the road. "Stop, Silas. Let me rest here."

He lowered me gently to the flat stone. He removed his *tallith*, and his hair flowed to his shoulders, like a stallion's mane. His teeth shone when he smiled at me. I felt I could confide in him.

"Silas, why did Jesus allow himself to be baptized? Gaius told me that it wasn't necessary, yet he submitted anyway."

"True. He didn't need to be purified, but he needed the people to see him as one chosen for righteousness. It was the beginning of his work of teaching and healing."

"If I got circumcised before setting out with you and Paul, would I be following his example?"

"You would. Paul told me you objected to circumcision. Have you thought any more about it?"

"All night. In the stables. It seems Jesus knows the goats as well as I do. I felt his presence. He spoke to me. I know that no sacrifice is too great to follow him. This morning, Amram's actions convinced me. When I heard his insults and felt his hatred, I knew that those like him, strict about the law, would never listen to Jesus' love from one who isn't circumcised. I'll do it."

Silas' raised an eyebrow and looked sideways at me. "And your father?"

"He won't understand." I took a deep breath, put both hands on my knee and pushed myself to my feet. My ankle was stiff and painful, but it bore my weight without more pain.

Silas supported me as I turned back toward Lystra.

"Where are you going?" he asked.

"To the carpentry. Help me, Silas, and when we get there, I want you to leave. I have to face him alone. He's a proud Greek and won't agree easily to the carving of my flesh."

It was still early when we reached Father's shop. The door was barred. Silas helped me open it and left me sitting on a stool to rest my ankle. I knew Father would be along soon, so I hopped about the shop and gathered a few pieces of wood and some tools. I fashioned a simple crutch that supported my weight well enough.

Gaius and Father would have to do without me at the ironworks. I'd be useless to them with my weak ankle.

It wasn't long before I heard noises from beyond the market square. When I peered through the doorway, I saw people stirring about and shouting. I hopped across the square on my crutch. At Kamilus' bakery, Kopries stopped me. He stretched his long arm out toward the people. "Timothy, there's been an accident at the ironworks"

"Father's there. Kopries, Come with me."

The crowd blocked the passage that led to Hiram and Jotham's ironworks two streets beyond. It was impossible to get past, but when I heard a man whisper, "Andreas," I panicked and swung my stick to force people away. I forgot about the pain in my foot and rushed on. Men and women stood about, gawking and squawking like geese. The burly shapes of Gaius and the blacksmiths bent over my father, lying on the ground.

I fell to my knees, pushed the men away and gripped Father's tunic. His lips were blue. No breath escaped his mouth. My tears dropped softly to the still body beneath me. I held his face in my hands and shook it from side to side.

"Father! Father," I cried. Still no breath, no gasping or rush of life-giving air into his body.

"He's gone," I whispered. "Gone." Never had one word held such finality. I'd never again hear his voice, feel his strong arm about me, know he was nearby when I needed him.

Kopries knelt and put his arm around me. "I'm so sorry, my friend."

"Timothy?" It was Gaius's voice.

I shook my head. "What? What happened?" I whispered. I couldn't grasp the truth that Father was dead. I'd lived under his strong protection all my life. Even though I was about to leave him, I thought he would always be here when I returned.

Gaius pointed to the hammer lying near the body. "He'd finished checking the new roof posts and picked up the sledge to smack the old ones away. I saw the whole thing. He swung the hammer back, but as he shifted it forward, he let go and clutched his chest as if he'd been struck with a sword. He dropped to the ground like a stone just as you see him now."

What has Jehovah done? Thoughts tumbled in my head, boulders rolling down a hillside. What about Mother and Grandmother? The journey with Paul, the farm, the carpentry?

Father is gone!

I stared at the ashen face beside me and gripped my tunic. With a torturous grunt, I ripped the cloth from collar to chest. I scooped dirt from the ground and poured it on my head. "Behold my sorrow! Behold my loss!" I said, covering my face with my hands.

Gaius turned to the crowd. "There's nothing for you to see here. Andreas the carpenter is at peace with his maker. His good deeds remain, and his family. Go back to your work."

They left slowly, quietly.

Hiram fetched a blanket from his shop and draped it over Father. He pulled me to my feet and gripped me in his powerful arms. "I'll bring your mother and grandmother, Timothy. We'll do all we can to help you through this." He hitched mules to his delivery wagon and goaded them on toward the farm.

"Wait!" I called. I wiped the tears from my face. "Hold your wagon. We'll take Father home."

Hiram and Gaius lifted Andreas' body into the back of the mule-cart.

I limped over to Kopries. "Find Gurdi and ask him to come?" He nodded and ran off toward Heracles' pottery.

"Gaius, I've left the carpentry open. Would you close and bar the door for me?"

Hiram and Jotham stayed with me while we waited. I leaned against my crutch and closed my eyes. Whatever the future held, I would live in the presence of Jesus. He came to me in the night. He would come in this morning hour. 'My loving presence is with you forever,' he had said. Never would his presence be more welcome than now.

Jotham went ahead to prepare Mother and Grandmother. When the men returned, I climbed onto the seat beside Hiram and as we moved away from the ironworks, I watched our shadow flow along the grass at the roadside. Gurdi was in the back of the wagon to steady the body and keep it covered. Kopries, and Gaius followed, accompanied by the mournful howls of Lystran women. I felt emptiness with every plodding step of Hiram's mules. What words could I find to comfort Mother and Grandmother?

Mother was waiting with Jotham outside the farm gate. She twisted the sash at her waist, reflecting the torment on her face. She ran to us, climbed in and knelt beside her husband. She gently removed the blanket. She gripped the edge of her *chiton* and violently tore it from neck to heart. I expected the keening howl of widowed grief but heard only weeping. Mother's shoulders shook until she took a deep breath and cupped Father's face in her hands. She kissed his cheek and stroked his hair, then lifted her hands to heaven and cried out:

> O my God, my soul is cast down within me.
> This poor soul cries, 'Hear me O Lord.'
> Be near to this broken heart. Repair my crushed spirit.

She put one hand on her loved one's chest and closed her eyes. I climbed from the driver's bench into the box and put my arms around her. She buried her tear-stained face in my breast, "He's gone, Timothy, and I don't know where he may be."

Her body shook with deep sobs and gasping breaths.

She was tiny and frail, not the strong mother who always knew what to do in the worst of times. Now I alone bore the responsibility for my family. Mother and Grandmother needed my comfort and care. My own grief could wait. I rubbed Mother's back and whispered, "Jesus, our master, will not forget Father's kindness. We'll see him again, Mother."

She stroked Father's cheek then placed the blanket over him. She turned to me and wiped her tears with her sleeve. She closed her eyes, took a deep breath and her face calmed.

She sat beside Father and braced herself. "I'm ready."

I climbed onto the seat beside Hiram. He gently goaded the mules forward into the farm courtyard. As we passed through the gate, Paul and Silas stood to one side of the cart. Grandmother and Rachel stood on the other, weeping and crying aloud. It was as if we bore a champion's body and they'd formed a reception of honor.

Fitting, I thought. Father's support allowed our band of believers to strengthen and he was the first of us to fall to the greatest enemy.

The wagon stopped in the center of the yard just as Kopries and Gurdi came through the gate. Rachel hurried to them. She wiped her tears as she spoke to Gurdi.

Mother climbed down from the cart. Grandmother came to her side and held her arm. She put her head on Mother's shoulder and stroked her back.

I followed them, putting as little weight as I could on my injured ankle.

Mother tucked her hair under her shawl and brushed her clothes straight. She stood back and faced our friends. "I will not wail or cry out. I won't grieve like someone who's lost her heart's love forever. I will see him again."

She held her hand out to Father's body. "Here lies Andreas of Lystra, a man of goodness and honor. May his soul reside in El Shaddai's place of eternal rest."

"El Shaddai, Mother," I asked. "God Almighty?"

"Yes, 'God of the mountains.' He'd like that. The women will prepare him for burial but I won't have him put in the Lystran *polyandrion*. I can't visit him where he's crowded among others in the common cave, where the cock crows to scare away demons and Kerberus guards the entrance to the underworld." Mother's face twisted and tears flowed. "No. Let me see him in the mountains. I'll mark his burial place with a dove of peace. Let the Spirit of Jehovah be present where my loved one lies."

Rachel came quickly to her. "Come within," she said. "You may not wail out loud, but you need a private place to grieve." She took Mother to the house.

Gurdi tugged my sleeve. "I know a place, beyond my shelter. A cave hidden among the trees on the hill. Prepare him. Bring him, Timothy. It's the right place for Andreas to rest."

I felt deep sadness, but I choked back my tears. "I want to see this place, but we need to bury him by nightfall. I can't get there and back on this ankle, and Mother needs me here. The burial site should be sanctified by prayer.

"Gaius, Paul, Silas, will you go with Gurdi?" I asked. "We'll follow after Father's body is prepared."

They agreed and the four of them hurried off. Gurdi led the way. His hair flipped side to side each time he turned to check that the others were following. It was all they could do to keep up with my little mountain-man. I knew he'd do his best for me.

The women of Lystra washed Father's body, anointed it with spices and perfumes and wrapped it in linen. We started south toward Gurdi's shelter. Mother, Grandmother and I sat in Hiram's wagon to steady the body and Rachel walked behind, a black shawl pulled over her head and face.

As we passed Lystra, men and women joined our little procession, including Heracles, Kamilus and others who had chosen to follow the Nazarene. Gurdi met us at the road and led us beyond his home to a place between two low hills thick with brush and trees. Hiram stopped the wagon.

We walked the short distance to the cave where Paul, Silas, and Gaius waited, and looked inside. The entrance was low and the inside sloped downward. Daylight extended only a short distance, but it showed a bare dirt floor already swept clean. My friends had been busy.

"Will this do, Mother?"

She turned and looked away from the cave-mouth. I followed her gaze. Through the narrow opening of the trail, the slope we'd climbed stretched out below us. In the distance was another, smaller hill and on it, our giant oak, standing alone against the graying sky.

She breathed deeply and looked down at the mossy ground, then up at the canopy of trees. "Fertile earth, incense of pine, balm of pure air. It's as if Jehovah himself had chosen this place."

Mother held my hands. She spoke to me in words just above a whisper, "Take him in. Say the prayers. He's earned his rest."

We stepped back so the men could move Father's shrouded body into the cave. Silas, Paul, and Gaius stood by the entrance, their palms up, their eyes closed. As Hiram and Jotham climbed out of the cave, a white bird flapped from a bush nearby. A dove. Just what Mother wanted. She gasped as it soared away.

"It's a sign," said Silas. Jesus' Spirit is present. Come, gather here. Paul has words of comfort for Andreas' family."

Our friends from Lystra gathered beside Hiram's wagon. Kopries, Gurdi and Rachel came and stood behind us. They placed their hands on our backs and shoulders and prayed in their mother tongues. Greek, Lycaonian and Aramaic joined in a jumble of syllables made melodic by the spirit of love they shared.

There hadn't been time to cover our grief with fresh, colorful clothes. Even Silas, Paul and Gaius wore work tunics. Silas stood tall beside his companions. He closed his eyes and his lips moved in silent prayer. Gaius's stocky body planted itself firmly on the ground, his eyes open and calm. Paul looked insignificant beside Silas' height and Gaius's might. But his trim beard and steady gaze showed strength and intelligence.

Paul stepped forward and raised his hands. "My friends, we've laid to rest Andreas of Lystra, husband of Eunice, father of Timothy and brother to us all. You've become a strong community of believers, in part because Andreas supported you and opened his home to you.

He yoked himself to the master in this way. He lived as if he believed in Jesus."

Paul clasped his hands together. "Some may wonder about his fate in the afterlife. Messiah's words give us confidence that Andreas is at peace. Listen to what Jesus said: "Come to me you who work and bear the struggles of life. I will give you rest. You who've stood in the track beside me, yoked together as oxen, have learned that my heart is soft and my way is loving. You're the ones who've found rest for your soul. Now you know that my yoke is easy and my burden is light."

Paul prayed, "May Jehovah guard this holy place and keep the soul of our loved one, Andreas, until Messiah returns and we're united with him. Give solace to his family and courage to follow you in the days ahead. God bless and keep each of us in life's journey. So be it, amen."

Some of the men stayed behind to pile stones over the cave-mouth against wild animals. Mother, Grandmother, Rachel and I climbed into the wagon. Hiram goaded his mules toward our farm and Paul and Gurdi walked alongside.

Paul broke the silence. "Timothy, now what will you do?"

That thought had been in my mind from the moment I saw Father lying breathless on the ground at the ironworks. Fickle fate had turned again. I must stay at home.

I shook my head and stared at the wagon's wooden floor. "Seven days to grieve, then work. The farm, the carpentry."

Mother held my hand. "Speak no more, Timothy. There's something you must know. Gurdi will tell you."

Gurdi skipped forward and put one hand on the wagon. He held on and walked as quickly as his short legs could carry him. He glanced at Rachel before answering. "Now, mother Eunice? So soon after ... after Andreas?"

Mother put her arm around Rachel and nodded at Gurdi. "Now, good friend. It must be now."

His black eyes met mine for a moment. His brow tightened, then he glanced at the ground and he massaged his mouth.

His words came like a trickle of water burbling over boulders. "Your father and I. We talked. He said it would be good. Very good, he said."

Grandmother hid her face in Mother's shoulder then peeked out like a girl from behind her Mother's apron. Her eyes laughed. A hint of a smile graced Mother's lips, but her brows quickly tightened again in sorrow. What secret did she share with Grandmother on a day of deep sadness?

"What would be good, Gurdi?" I asked. "Tell me, my friend. I trust you."

My little friend looked at me. His dark eyebrows danced up and down, first opening his face in boldness, then tightening in doubt. "Rachel's father disowned her," he said. "She is under Andreas's roof. He is responsible. Said I could marry her."

I was stunned. Grandmother hid behind Mother's sleeve and again, the little smile briefly crossed Mother's face.

"I didn't know," I said. Then I remembered the day only a few weeks after Rachel had been beaten. Paul had persuaded Rachel to show her face. When Gurdi saw her, in spite of the scars, he'd said she was beautiful. And today, he'd stayed close by her, even now, walking on her side of the wagon. How could I have missed the love between them? I'd been eaten up by my own nightmare and like a mule wearing blinders, didn't see.

"Hiram," I said. "Stop the wagon."

I climbed out and limped around to Gurdi. I held his hand and took Rachel's also.

"I'm so happy for you. You have my blessing. May Jehovah bind you together as one and fill you with his love." I placed Rachel's hand in Gurdi's.

They looked at each other. Rachel's eyes shone. Gurdi swallowed hard and slowly turned to look at me.

"There's more," he said. "Andreas told me. You are going with Paul. I should take your place. Live on the farm. With Rachel."

What could I say? Father had said he'd find someone to take my place, but now that it was done, I felt I'd been let loose like a goat from its pen. Mother didn't need me. Another could take my place, had taken my place. I looked at Mother.

She took my hand and pressed it tightly. "You're free to go, my son."

Paul came along side. "You have much to think about, Timothy, and need time to grieve. Silas and I will stay in Lystra while you mourn and heal. Then our journey will begin. You may yet join us. Listen to Jesus' voice."

He gave my shoulder a squeeze. "Send Gaius when you have news," he said. Then he and Silas walked away.

I watched the men disappear through the gates of Lystra and remembered Jesus' voice from that morning: "All who tread this earth are precious to me. My presence is with you forever." Though it seemed liked days had passed, it had been only hours since I decided to be circumcised and go with Paul. Should I let today's terrible events change a decision I believed was right?

"We need to be together," I said. "To talk, to weep, to know El Shaddai's comfort."

I climbed back into the wagon. I put my arms around Mother and Grandmother, the women who had taught me since childhood to trust Jehovah's ways.

"Hiram," I called. "Take us home."

In spite of our grief, the days flew by. Paul circumcised me, and he and Silas stayed until I was fully healed. Under Gaius training, Gurdi would learn enough to keep the shop running and, if he showed sufficient talent, would fare well.

As for me, I was about to venture into a world of marketplaces and synagogues full of people who knew no love like Jesus'. That love dwelt deep in my heart. On the road, I'd be free of home's restraints, free to show what Messiah's love could do.

PART II

ICONIUM

Paul and his companions travelled through the region of Phrygia and Galatia. Acts 16:6

9

Via Sebaste

WE PACKED LATE INTO THE NIGHT. OUR NEIGHBORS AND FRIENDS HAD provided more than we needed for our travel. Hiram and Jotham gave me their best mule to carry our gear. I named her Ruth, trusting that she'd be as faithful as her namesake. Grandmother made sure I had cooking utensils and dishes. She tried to make me take more, but the packs and cart held only so much.

I took Father's best gear. Sturdy footwear, a sharp knife, leather bags, new wineskins and a few carpentry tools. We had figs, cheese wine and bread to get us as far as Iconium.

On the day we left, I woke early and went to the stable to feed the animals for the last time. Grandmother was there, talking softly to the kids. She was sitting on a three-legged milking stool and turned when she heard my footsteps. Wisps of white hair curled from under her shawl and wrinkles creased her face as she smiled. "I thought you'd be along soon, my darling boy."

I squatted beside her and kissed her on the cheek. "Grandmother."

She held my head in her hands. "My little lamb," she said, "a few moments with you before the day takes you away. This is a quiet place at dawn and I knew you'd come. You'll miss your friends of the stable, Timothy. These creatures love the boy who feeds them, just as we love the Father who feeds us."

"I'll miss you, Nana. Part of me doesn't want to leave."

She kissed me again and I sat on the floor beside her. "You're a strong young man," she said, "and the ancient wisdom is a seed within you. It will burst and grow. It will flourish in your life. Remember Solomon, 'Listen closely to my words, for they are life to whose who find them and health to a man's whole body.'"

We fed the animals together that morning, as we'd done when I was a boy. We chatted like old women, remembering years gone by, treasures of love stored in jars of clay.

When we were done we crossed to the kitchen. Mother had prepared boiled eggs with goat cheese, barley bread, olives and figs. An amphora of fresh water stood in the middle of the table. The heat from the cooking fire took off the morning chill. We sat and held hands across the table while I prayed a simple blessing.

Mother kept hold of my hand. She looked steadily at me. "My son, my love. Today you leave us, and we may not see you again." Her lips creased in a thin smile. "We'll pray Isaiah's words for you every day:

May the God of Abraham and Isaac go before you, bless and keep you.
May he prepare the path before you.
May your feet be shod with the gospel of peace.

"You will take Jesus' words to those who don't have his love. Leave us, knowing our love goes with you forever."

I pulled them into a strong embrace. "Of all the gifts I've been given for this journey, your love is the one I need the most. I couldn't go without your blessing, and knowing you're cared for." I kissed each of them.

"Now, I hear people in the courtyard. It's time." We went out into the bright sun.

Paul and Silas had packed Ruth and the cart ready for travel. Rachel put an amphora of fresh water in the cart, then stood beside Gurdi.

Gurdi pressed a leather bag into my hands.

"Take this. Take it, Timothy. It's from your friends. It will help you do Jesus' work where we cannot go."

I shook his hand and hugged him. "Thank you, Gurdi. May God bless you in Lystra. Serve him well, my friend. I'll never forget you."

"Timothy," Gaius said. "I've been praying for this since Paul first told me he was looking for a young man to go with him. Now God's prepared you and he'll be with you. Serve him well, my brother."

"Keep praying," I said. "Without that, I'd certainly fail."

He handed me a wooden disk on a leather string. "Take this with you."

I read the words inscribed on it: *fides, spes, caritas. Faith, hope, love.* On the other side only one word: *semper.* Always.

I smiled and hugged Gaius. "I'll treasure this. It will be my strength. Thank you."

He clapped me on the shoulder. "Now, get on your way. I want to see the back of you. Gurdi and I have work to do," he said, and laughed.

I turned to our mule and wagon. "Farewell," I said. It was the hardest parting I had ever experienced.

We set our footsteps toward Iconium and fell silent as we walked. Not far from Lystra, I let Silas take Ruth's reins and I ran along the horse path at the roadside. I felt strong and steadily increased my speed until I flew across the ground like Pegasus. I loved the wind in my hair, caressing my body and ruffling my tunic. What would it be like to run as athletes do, competing for a prize?

Eventually I turned back and found Paul and Silas near the bottom of a steep hill. I tucked my dreams away in a private corner of my mind.

I leaned against the wagon and looked toward Iconium. The travelers ahead trudged a weary line straight toward the city.

The Via Sebaste separated the lightly treed hills and mountains to the west and north from the vast, green plain to the east. Rabbi

Shemuel taught that after the flood, survivors favoured the high ground, but the centuries since had been free from the wrath of God and the city spread into the plain where lush farmlands prospered. It was now an ancient, sprawling trade centre.

"It's a crowded city, my friends," Paul said. "On our first visit, after we preached in the synagogue, many came to follow Jesus, but Shemuel stirred up others who forced us out of the city. We still have friends among both the Greek and the Jews, but enemies as well."

"We won't approach the synagogue this time, but teach only in trusted homes. I don't know if my brittle bones can stand another beating."

"He took a savage beating in Lystra, Silas," I said. "I thought he was dead. We can't let it happen again."

Silas bit the side of his lip and nodded. He placed the amphora in the wagon and took our mule's reins. "Whatever is waiting for us in Iconium, it's within sight. Let's be off."

10

WITHIN THE HOUR, THE SUN HAD SET AND THE AIR COOLED. ICONIUM'S walls loomed before us.

We followed in the wake of other travelers. With our wagon open to inspection, our small party passed easily through the gate. The colossal statue of Perseus stood in the centre of the town square. A fearsome dragon's head hung from Perseus' strong right hand.

Silas pointed to the massive icon that gave Iconium its name. "Jupiter's son protects this city, but only Jehovah's son can free it."

Just then a small man with a fringe of short hair strode toward us. He wore a white tunic with a braided belt. It was Petronius, attendant to Julian Eutychus, who was an important clerk in the provincial government. Julian had spent a few weeks in Lystra the year before, teaching us.

"Timothy! Paul!" he called. "I've been waiting for you. Gaius sent a messenger two days ago with news of your coming. We thought you'd be here late today, or early tomorrow."

Petronius embraced Paul and looked at Silas. "Who is this?"

"This is Silas, our brother and partner in faith," Paul said. "He's well known in Jerusalem and is also beloved in Derbe and Lystra for his stories of the Nazarene."

Petronius' eyes widened. "You knew Jesus? You looked into his eyes and listened to his voice? You must share with us."

"You can be sure of it, my friend," Silas said. "My love for the master grows stronger every time I tell his story."

"Your words will be water on parched ground." Petronius put his hands together. "My master, Julian, instructed me to offer you the hospitality of his home as long as you wish to stay. Come, I'll show you the way."

Before long, we entered a square with a fountain in its centre. Petronius straightened his tunic. "Look beyond this square. There's Julian's house."

He pointed to a large house lit by torches along the wall. Petronius led us to a gate at the side of the property where a slave took care of our mule and wagon. Then he took us inside and went to announce our arrival. Frescoes of woodlands and streams decorated the atrium's walls and floor. Strong incense, an eastern scent, reminded me of a temple. Julian came immediately. He was almost my height and lean. His face was broad with a wide-mouthed smile and blunt, spaced teeth. He bowed deeply to Paul.

"It's my honour to welcome you, my friend and teacher, and those who travel with you, Timothy, Silas. Stay as long as you wish. Petronius! Quickly, water for their feet, food and wine for their refreshment."

"Julian," I said. "Mother and Grandmother send their greetings. We miss your teaching and now you offer your hospitality. We're in your debt."

"No, Timothy, we owe each other nothing. Our debt is to the master only. God gives. It's my duty to share his goodness. You're always welcome."

He took me by both arms. "Gaius' messenger told us of Andreas' death," he said softly. "We've prayed for you, Timothy. Your mother and grandmother are well, I hope."

"I left them under Gaius' care."

"Then they're in the best hands." He turned and led us to a semicircular room. We sat in marble seats shaded by a dome.

"When I was in Lystra," Julian said, "you were praying for your Jewish brothers. Are they still opposing you?"

"They've banished us from their worship," I said. "Our dear friend Rachel? Her own father beat her almost to death. She'll bear the scars forever."

"But the master is working, Julian," Paul added. "His followers influence the whole town with their good deeds."

As he spoke, two women entered, draped in flowing garments. They glided to Julian and he held their hands. The older wore a sky-blue gown, a stola. The younger woman's stola was perfumed in a lovely coastal scent like lavender. Her hair danced in ringlets down her back. They draped her slender neck and framed her petite face. Her eyes, black as the darkest onyx, were full of life, and mischievous, maybe not quite ready for formal society. A pair of gold fibulae, shaped like a cat stalking an unsuspecting bird, pinned her garment together at each shoulder.

Julian introduced us to his wife, Macaria and daughter Cassandra. I felt conspicuous in their presence, dusty and unwashed from travel.

"Please," Macaria said, "Take your rest. I know you're tired, but let us talk for a while then you can refresh yourselves in your rooms."

Cassandra bowed and left us as Petronius entered with two slaves carrying basins of water. One put his basin on the floor in front of me and I eased my dusty feet into the water. I let the cool freshness soak in while the slave massaged my feet then dried them vigorously with a sheepskin. Servants brought bread, wine, olives, and succulent figs which must have been kept over the winter in a cooling cellar.

"Julian," Paul asked, "Tell me how the believers are doing here. Have they been faithful to my teaching?"

"We've had some trouble. Rabbi Shemuel, stirs up his people to harass the Jewish Christians. He bars them from the synagogue and they're shunned, just as in Lystra." Julian held his goblet out to the slave to be refilled.

"But," Macaria said, "they've gained both fellowship and business with us and it almost makes up for the lack. We women talk with them in the market and they tell us Jehovah is good. We've lost a few who couldn't endure the persecution. They still believe in Jesus, but they worship in their old faith."

She rose from beside Julian. "Excuse me. I must see to the cooking."

"God is good," said Julian, "but we need more teaching, Paul. What do you have for us?"

"We'll teach here in your home, rather than in the public square or the synagogue. I don't want to cause more hostility. You must be strong. There will be opposition. It's our calling."

"Of course," said Julian. "I'll have Petronius pass the word that you'll teach tomorrow night."

Julian turned to Silas and gripped his arm. "Forgive me. I'm so eager for Paul's news that I've neglected you. You honour my home with your presence."

"And it's my privilege to meet you, Julian. Your faith is known as far as Antioch. Paul's made sure of it." Silas winked.

"Ah, but you must watch him," said Julian. "He only tells the good parts. We'll talk while you're here, as brothers."

Macaria entered the room and interrupted our conversation. "Servillius is back with eggs and goat's milk. Cook has roasted hare and baked bread. We have a feast ready. Come, let's enjoy God's provision."

From behind Macaria, Cassandra crossed the room directly to me, took me by the hand and invited me to the dining room. Her fingers sat light as feathers in mine. I felt I was holding a fragile treasure and was embarrassed by the familiarity. Macaria had done the same with Paul and Silas so I assumed it was a family custom.

Darkness had closed in. Oil lamps flickered on the walls against colorful frescoes of meadows, lakes and wildlife. We reclined, in the Roman style, on couches soft as meadow-moss, not lumpy with straw.

Cassandra's lashes flashed and her deep black eyes drew me in like eddies of dark water. She smiled, "Father has told me about you."

Her blunt statement made me seem dangerous, someone not to be trusted.

"He said you're the leader of the church in Lystra. But, you're young. Not yet twenty, I think."

As she spoke, she picked a fig from the platter and turned it in her slender fingers. She raised it slowly to her mouth and wrapped her ripe lips around its purple skin. She scooped the flesh from the fruit with pearl-white teeth. A single drop of juice fell on her chin, which she gently wiped away. My eyes were glued to her. I'd never been in such an intimate setting, nor so close to a beauty like this.

A hint of frown crossed Cassandra's brow. "Are you, Timothy?"

Her lips moved, but the words hardly reached my sluggish brain. "Am I what?" I asked, stupidly. I picked up a piece of boiled egg on bread and tried to eat without drawing attention to myself.

Her eyebrows arched. "Are you yet twenty?"

"No, not twenty." I struggled over what to say next. One vision filled my mind and I spoke without thinking.

"You're very beautiful."

She laughed aloud. Not a polite giggle, but a joyous laugh. Conversation stopped. Macaria cocked her head toward her daughter. Julian lifted his head and sniffed. Paul and Silas looked curiously at her.

Cassandra covered her eyes. "Forgive me. Please don't let it spoil your meal. I'll be more discreet." She couldn't prevent a tiny giggle from escaping her lips. Then she pressed them tightly together and took a deep breath.

"Oh dear," she whispered, and looked at me like a misbehaving youngster.

"You're an imp," I said.

She turned away, but not before I caught the glint in her eyes. Her humour and mischief melted the social divide I'd felt. I admired her casual assurance, but I couldn't copy it out of respect for the others.

I nodded toward Paul and Silas. "Aren't you uneasy in the presence of these great teachers?"

She tore a piece of bread from the platter. "I know Paul. When he taught in this house, I was a spoiled girl. I loved the beautiful gardens and rich food. I had playthings, a pony and cart, but I thought there had to be something more to life than riches. Inside, I was empty. I didn't know what it meant until Paul came. He told us what Jesus taught. He made me think."

Cassandra swallowed a morsel of bread and tore a piece of tender roast hare from its carcass.

"About emptiness?" I asked.

She waved the hare's leg in lazy circles near her mouth. "No, about fullness. Jesus said that those who follow him would live life to the full." She raised both hands. "That's what I want. Not a life watching over slaves in a house of plenty. I want to change things."

I thought about my friends in Lystra. Each of them had been changed.

"I want to change people," I said. It slipped from my mouth as if spoken by someone else. It was then I became aware of the purpose of my life. It had hibernated in my mind waiting for the right moment to emerge, like ground squirrels in the spring.

"That's it! You said it, Timothy." Cassandra nearly shouted. "We have the same mind, you and I. We want to change people, not things."

She turned to Paul. "Isn't that right? Doesn't Jesus call us to change people, as Timothy says?"

I looked toward Paul and became aware that we had everyone's attention. Even Petronius was looking at us with his mouth agape, holding a pitcher of wine over Julian's outstretched goblet.

Paul propped himself on one elbow to face us. He wiped his mouth and cleared his throat. Then came the pursed lips that made his goatee merge with his moustache, like shutters closing a window. Before he spoke, he moved his head just a touch from side to side. I knew we were about to receive words of correction from Jesus' disciple.

"There's only one who can transform the lives of those who live for worldly satisfactions," he said. "Not you. Not I. Only the Nazarene. But you do well, young ones, to see that Jesus wishes all men and women to change. Now, learn how the master might use you to help him change people. Then you'll live life to the full."

Paul turned to Julian and Cassandra. "It's time for us to retire. We're enriched by your hospitality and we thank you."

Julian stood. "Petronius will show you to your rooms. Sleep well."

I thanked Julian and Macaria for the evening's fare and followed Petronius. I glanced back. As Cassandra turned away, she looked over her shoulder at me. She smiled and raised one eyebrow, like an old friend signaling future adventures together.

Paul leaned toward me. "You've made a friend, Timothy. Be wary."

I didn't understand.

"It's about women, Timothy," Silas said. "None accompanied the apostle on his first journey."

When I'd committed to travelling with Paul, I didn't consider that women would be part of it. As I fell asleep that night, I realized that I could be nothing more than Cassandra's friend. That fact was tested by the memory of her soft, slender fingers resting in my hand.

My farm-boy habits woke me at dawn next morning. I thought I should keep some distance from Cassandra. Cook served a light breakfast and when Julian came, I offered to work on his coaches.

"I'd be a poor host to ask that of a guest, Timothy. Take your rest today. Paul will have work for you tonight, I believe."

"I'm not good at rest, sir. There was no time for it at home. Paul believes it's the master's will that his servants owe no man anything."

"Then take Petronius with you. He oversees my property."

Petronius led me through the garden to an open portico at the back. Our cart sat alongside a three-harness chariot, a *triga*, carefully crafted and decorated with handsome paintings of horses and athletes. It must have been an impressive sight when Julian took his family out on a formal occasion. It rivaled the fanciest coaches I'd seen on the road to Iconium.

"I've never seen such a skillful work of carpentry," I said to Petronius. "It doesn't want my clumsy, farm-carpenter hands working on it."

While Petronius watched, I turned to our humble cart. The wheels were wearing along the rims, but not so badly they needed much attention, although I did a little shaping with an adze to even out the rough spots. The hub and axle were also in good shape.

"How many days to Antioch, Petronius?"

"With your mule and cart, not more than ten."

"Then I'll do no more today. The cart will hold together until Antioch."

Petronius began putting tools away just as Paul and Silas entered the portico.

"Now, Timothy. I have work for you," Paul said. Will you tell your story tonight for the believers?"

"Well, yes, of course, Paul. What should I say?"

"Tell them what you've seen and heard and felt. The Spirit will be your guide, if you pray and trust him."

"Then I'll go and pray. Thank you for trusting me."

"No, no, my son. It's not you I trust, it's the powerful God you serve. I see his strength in you. You must trust him!"

We gathered that night in the largest space in Julian's home, the airy and fresh atrium garden. Forty or fifty people crowded into the space. Cassandra and her mother sat on cushions by a small shrub. I was very nervous.

Paul and Silas stood at the top of the stairs that led down to the garden. Paul called on me to speak and my legs turned to rubber. My hands sweat and shook like leaves in the wind. My throat turned dry as dust.

When I reached Paul, he put his arm around my shoulder and whispered in my ear, "God has not given the Spirit of fear, my son, but of confidence and a sound mind. Take a breath, be calm."

While he prayed, my senses returned and the room came back into view. I felt confident even though my voice quavered with my first few words.

"My tame is Nimothy," I said. There was a ripple of laughter. "Ah, Timothy, I should say. I'm sorry. You're the biggest crowd I've ever spoken to."

"It's all right, Nimothy," Julian said and the laughter returned. "We're all friends here. Tell us what happened in Lystra."

I took a breath and spoke in a bold voice so even those at the back could hear.

"Miracles happened in Lystra," I said. "My friend Kopries, a cripple, who'd never taken a step in his life, walked when Jesus strengthened his legs.

"Today, Kopries feeds the hungry at the city gate. He works in the market. He tells people what God has done for him. He's a leader in the church. He walks in the steps of our master and that's what convinced me to follow Jesus. I've been circumcised so I can speak in the synagogue."

Why did I say that in front of all those people? I glanced at Cassandra. She was staring at her hands. Maybe she hadn't heard.

"When Father died," I went on, "it changed me. Jesus made everything right so I could follow him with Paul and Silas. He brought people into our family to take my place. Gurdi to do the carpentry and Gaius to teach him, and Rachel. Oh, let me tell you about Rachel.

"She's the only Jewish woman in Lystra who'll be friends with Mother. She was beaten near to death by her father and husband because she follows Jesus. The scars still mark her, but Messiah has turned their ugliness to beauty. And he's given her a husband, a home, a good life. That's what it is to follow Jesus. Our ugliness is turned to beauty. Our death is turned to life."

Suddenly, the words stopped coming. I turned to Silas. "Isn't that right, Silas?" I asked.

"It's true," he said. "In Jerusalem, I saw the Pharisees refuse to believe that Jesus had healed a blind man even though they'd seen it with their own eyes. Timothy saw the miracles in Lystra and bears witness to their truth. It's the same truth for Hebrew and Gentile."

Paul stepped forward and invited them to come back the next day. He dismissed the meeting with a prayer of blessing. "May the grace of the master, and the love of God and the fellowship of the Spirit be with you all."

As people began to leave, a young man took my arm. Tight curls covered his head. "My name is Orestes," he said. "I see that you're sincere and honest, but why would you worship one god when you can worship all the gods? How could your way possibly be better?"

Cassandra had found me by that time and answered him. "Well, what have your gods done for you lately?"

He crossed his arms and faced Cassandra. "Nothing, but what's got that to do with it?"

"Everything. Jesus is always present," she said, "He talks with me, comforts me, guides me, like a friend. When grandfather fell down a rocky hillside and died last month, the master dried my tears, comforted me and was with me through the pain. Do your gods do that?"

"The gods are above our common lives. You know that."

"I do," said Cassandra. "They never helped me in the past, but when I turned to Jesus, everything changed. You can have the same close friendship with him that I have. Do you want to?"

He paused and looked at the floor, shaking his head a little as if he wondered whether he was about to make a big mistake. His answer surprised me.

"Cassandra, I've watched you. I see you've changed. I want that too. Tell me how."

The tension in his face relaxed and a little smile developed around his lips. I was getting edgy as I listened. I wanted to join in, but I bit my tongue and let Cassandra continue.

"Jesus died and came back from the grave," she said, "and he is the only way to God. Orestes, his miracles prove what he claimed. Believe this and follow him. Your life will change."

"Then let God change my life," Orestes said. "I'll follow the way of Jesus. But you must teach me, Cassandra."

"We'll teach you," Cassandra said glancing at me. "Can we come and see you tomorrow?"

"Yes, of course. Come after sunset when I'll be finished my work."

"We'll have to come before sunset," Cassandra said. "I can't be out after dark. God be with you, Orestes."

Orestes bowed, thanked Cassandra and moved toward the courtyard doorway.

Cassandra had been a whirlwind that blew in, swept the situation up and left everything changed. She was remarkable.

I was caught up in the twister myself. Cassandra was staring at me, her eyes wide and her hands clasped in glee.

"Wasn't that exciting?" She said. "I've known Orestes almost all my life and this is the first time he's come to one of our meetings. I've been asking him for a good six months. It was your talk that opened his eyes tonight. Amazing things come from simple trust and honesty. You're a blessing to us, Timothy. I'll find you tomorrow so we can go to Orestes' farm."

She left as quickly as she'd come, still bubbly with excitement and encouraging everyone she passed.

Good Lord, how could I ignore such a tornado?

II

Kybele

I woke up to a bird chirping nearby. At first I thought I was outdoors, but when I opened my eyes, rather than a lofty blue sky I saw my cubicle's geometric, bordered walls. I rubbed my eyes and looked through the doorway. A small brown bird strutted on stubby toes by the atrium pool. It chirped a cheerful song and raised the feathers on its head, like a turban. When I lowered my feet to the floor, it faced me. The feathers on its throat swelled with song then it flew away through the open atrium roof. Birdsong to start the day, I thought. What could be better?

I pulled on my tunic, splashed water on my face from the atrium well, then sat beside the pool and wondered about the upcoming visit with Orestes. It didn't seem right that Cassandra had shown no reservations at all about wandering the countryside with me. Young women in Lystra weren't allowed such freedom. It wasn't my concern, I thought. She'd have to sort it out with her parents. I heard Paul's moaning yawn from his cubicle behind me and turned to see him walking gingerly, toward the well.

"My limbs are like stone and the ankles burn until I've taken a few steps," he complained.

He washed his face and balding head then carefully shaped his greying goatee. His beard was a reflection of his character. It was tightly clipped and he stroked or combed it with his fingers when he talked or prepared to answer a question or give instruction. He placed his hand on my shoulder as he lowered himself to sit by the pool's edge.

Petronius moved briskly down the hall with Julian and nodded toward the front door. Julian greeted us hastily and excused himself to go to his tablinum where he'd meet his clients. I assumed they were at the door waiting for Petronius to let them in.

Macaria arrived and invited us to light refreshment. We moved into the dining room. Cassandra reclined on the dining couch, holding a cluster of grapes in front of her closed eyes. She groaned as she forced them open and lazily moved her gaze to us. "Ah," she said, and yawned. "Our guests. Forgive me, I'm not quite awake."

Less a woman and more a child early in the day, I thought. She seemed an unpretentious girl, comfortable with people in any situation. I felt calmed by her presence and wanted to be near her, but Macaria positioned herself between us. We reclined at the table where eggs, cheese, figs and fruit were displayed on polished silver platters.

Macaria pointed to the glass ewers of water. "It's fresh from the mountain brooks, brought each morning." A servant poured cups of the sweet water.

"Timothy," Macaria asked, "where did you find the courage to leave your mother and grandmother to go with Paul?"

"Jehovah showed me this is what he wants me to do. There could be no other way. I wonder, myself, where the strength came from."

"Sometimes," Paul said, "we know the leading of the master without question. Other times, it takes real effort. We learn discernment from both experiences."

"Macaria," I asked, "Would you let Cassandra go on such a journey?" Cassandra's brows lifted and her face flushed with excitement. I marveled that she kept silent.

A shadow of alarm crossed her mother's face. "With you?"

"No, no, of course not. Well, I mean, not that I wouldn't want that.

I mean, oh goodness, I don't know what I mean. Please, forgive me. What I wondered was, how does a parent feel about a child leaving home?"

I could feel my cheeks burning, and didn't dare look at anyone else. I locked eyes with Macaria until she seemed uncomfortable and looked away.

"Well, of course, any parent has some anxiety about their child's safety and their future. I would certainly miss Cassandra, but I don't think of such a possibility. After all, Cassandra is still a child. When she's a woman she'll be expected to keep house, not travel the world."

"I guess that's why I ask," I said. "When Jesus gave his great challenge to go into all the world and make disciples, was he speaking to women as well as men? Surely, women are as capable of spreading the gospel as men. And they'd be more effective taking the news to other women than men would be."

"That's right!" Cassandra said. "I love teaching Jesus' truth. I want to preach to a multitude, like he did."

I could feel Macaria stiffen beside me. "Cassandra, just as it's inappropriate for women to serve in the Senate, it's inappropriate for them to lecture crowds of men. Please put such thoughts out of your mind. Paul, surely you have something to say about this." She looked at Paul and jerked her head toward Cassandra, pleading for his support.

"Yes, I do," Paul answered. He spoke carefully, aware of the tension. "Among Jews, just as among Romans, the father is head of the home. Women take care of the household, as you say, Macaria. They do not address crowds. When I began serving the master, I went to the synagogues where I'd be recognized and invited to teach. When they rejected me, I preached in the marketplace and found, to my surprise, that gentiles accepted the truth and became followers."

Paul held his goblet up and the slave filled it then served the rest of us. Cassandra stopped eating and propped her chin on both hands to listen to Paul. The sun had risen and it shone through the atrium roof into nearly every corner of the house. It sharpened the umber and forest green walls in the dining room and highlighted the glistening moisture on the grapes. I picked a few and enjoyed their sweetness. Silas started peeling his third egg.

Paul took a deep breath and smiled wryly. "Things are not as they used to be. Jesus has brought a new way. The good news is not for the Jew alone, though Jesus was a Jew. It is not for men alone, though Jesus was a man. Perhaps a time will come when the gospel will not be preached only by Jews, or only by men. But for now, to stir up as little opposition as possible, we must follow the customs of our time and of the place we're in. Let men preach to the crowds. Let women speak to one here and one there, and the master will bless every time a seed is planted."

"Very sensible," Macaria said. She turned to Cassandra and nodded.

Cassandra pouted and looked at her mother sideways. She struck me as the most beautiful woman I'd ever seen.

"There is something I must add," Paul said, as he stood to leave. "I think for purely practical purposes, that men should remain unmarried if they're to travel and spread the truth. Wives and family can be a distraction. Jesus said, 'Those who leave home, or brothers or sisters or mother or father or children for me and the good news will receive a hundred times as much in this present age and in the age to come, eternal life.' I believe the master was commending a solitary life, given to the gospel. I'm not saying it's the only way, but it's the most effective.

"Now, Macaria, Cassandra, please excuse us. Once again, we've been refreshed by your hospitality and your inquisitive spirits. Let's rejoice in what God is doing. Whether rich or poor, man or woman, we brought nothing into this world and we can take nothing out. So, having food and clothing, let's be content."

We left the women standing in the dining room. I glanced back to see Macaria talking to her daughter while wagging one finger at her. I imagined what she might be saying and realized that I, too, must address some awkward issues.

The atrium held a small line of men waiting to see Julian. One of them, a full-faced, heavy-set man lifted his head and smiled when he saw Silas.

"That's Silvanus," Silas said. "We talked last night and I know he has more questions. Paul, Timothy, excuse me." He hurried to Silvanus and shook his hand warmly.

I walked with Paul to the garden. "Paul," I said, "last night, Cassandra and I arranged to meet with a young man, Orestes, to teach him about following Jesus. We'll be late to the evening meeting, but we should be able to bring Orestes."

"Timothy, keep in mind that the master may have a special purpose for Orestes. Your influence on him will be timely. If he's been rescued from darkness, he must be taught how to walk in the light. The most formative times in learner's lives are those spent with a mature disciple."

"And of course," Paul said, "You must seek Julian's permission."

"About Cassandra?" I asked.

He stroked his beard. "It's not customary for young women to have such freedom. Don't be alone with her. Take Petronius and a female servant to chaperone. Julian will insist on that at least. We'll be here in Iconium only a few more days and then we'll be gone for a year or more as the master leads. There will be time for you to learn his plan. Be patient."

We left the garden. I noticed there was no one in the atrium, so I looked for Julian in his tablinum. He was instructing Petronius about the evening meeting. As always, the slave took instructions graciously and hastened away.

"Well, that's taken care of," he said and turned to me.

"No more clients this morning?" I asked.

"Done for now," He said. "How was your meal, Timothy?"

"Very fine. You're a wonderful host, Julian."

He began to tidy some documents on his desk.

"I see you're busy," I said, "but I must ask you about this afternoon."

He stopped and looked at me. "Of course. Please continue."

"Last night Orestes asked Cassandra and me to come to his farm and tell him more about Jesus. I've come to seek your permission and advice."

He stood and adjusted his toga. "Rightfully so. This is no simple decision, young man. Did Cassandra agree to this, ah, adventure?" He rested on the corner of his writing desk and motioned for me to sit on the chair nearby.

"Yes," I said. "In fact, she suggested it when Orestes asked how he could learn more."

"It's not at all acceptable for Cassandra to go with you alone."

A large woman, a household servant, passed by. Julian called to her. "Servilia, come here." He tossed a drooping fold of his toga over his shoulder and looked at me. "Let me reduce the possibility of harm. You must have Petronius and Servilia, accompany you. She is mature, known throughout the community for her strict standards. That should keep the tongues from wagging."

"Thank you," I said as I rose from my chair.

"Servilia," he said. "You will accompany Cassandra this afternoon. She will tell you what to do."

Servilia bowed and left.

I turned toward the door, but Julian took my arm. "Keep in mind, Timothy, that Cassandra is betrothed to Appion, a prominent local administrator. He would not take kindly to any mishap or embarrassment. Be discreet."

"I will. Thank you." I stumbled back toward the door, tripping slightly over my feet, as I tried to conceal my surprise.

Cassandra was betrothed! My heart sank with the realization, but I resolved to bury my feelings and resist all further affection for Cassandra. It seemed, after all, that her friendliness to me was no different than the attention she showed to others. The special attraction I thought we had? I must have imagined it.

12

Castratio

WITH PETRONIUS AS PROTECTOR AND SERVILIA AS CHAPERONE, WE arrived at Orestes' farm near the end of day. He was bent over, scratching a piglet's chin as he poured water into a depression in the ground.

"Orestes," I called. When he turned, the sun shone on his rugged, sweaty chest. I saw Cassandra look at him, her eyes enticingly visible above her veil.

"I see you've worked all day." Her voice danced with mischief. "Are you ready to play?"

She was as flirtatious with Orestes as she'd been with me when we first met.

"By the gods, yes!" he replied. He pulled a tunic over his torso. "Let's explore my domain."

Hadn't we come to talk about Orestes' newfound faith? I felt left out and that Cassandra was reckless, but I remembered how effective she'd been in our first conversation with Orestes.

I shrugged my shoulders and gestured for Orestes to lead on, trusting that Cassandra knew what she was doing.

He threw a bag over his shoulder and started out, like Pan leading a flock through newly ploughed fields. The piglet sniffed my boots and tugged at Cassandra's cloak.

"Flatface," Orestes growled. He smacked her on the rear and the agile little porker bobbed up and down as her feet propelled her along.

"I've fed that runt since birth," he said. "She follows me everywhere."

"How will you part with this one when it's time for slaughter?" I asked.

Orestes laughed. "She'll be someone's dinner one day. I'm fulfilling her purpose. It's a loss, but there'll be another to take her place."

The stony path turned up a scrubby hillside. The plain of Iconium stretched toward the horizon where Black Mountain stood.

Flatface scurried among the folds of Cassandra's gown. "Ooh," she cried, then she snatched the piglet up, holding her at arm's length. "If being someone's dinner is this lowly animal's purpose," she said, "then, surely you have a purpose, Orestes. What is it?"

Flatface wriggled as if in protest and almost squirmed out of Cassandra's grip. Orestes grabbed the pig and held it in one arm while scratching its belly. Flatface's eyes closed in bliss.

"To be honest," he said, "before last night, I'd never really thought of it, but it's been in my head all day. Last night I bowed to Jesus. He's my God, but I don't know what that means in my life. How do I serve him?"

Cassandra turned to me. "Timothy, tell Orestes what it means for you to serve Jesus. You've left your home to travel with Paul."

I swallowed, trying to subdue my feelings. Every time I heard her voice or looked into her eyes, I was drawn in. I couldn't shake the feeling that we belonged to one another. Move on, I told myself. Be a brother, not a lover. I forced my heart to be calm.

"Cassandra's right, Orestes. I'm with Paul to help, but I'm still learning."

Flatface tired of Orestes attention and nearly wriggled out of his arms. Orestes set the piglet on the ground. The sun's last rays stretched its shadow to look like a racing dog as she brushed past the folds of Servilius' dress and snuffled about on the rocky path.

I pointed to Flatface. "It's like your piglet," I said. "Instead of squirming like that, the learner must be still and let the master speak. Then he'll know the teaching and where God leads. What did your father say about your decision to follow Jesus?"

He looked toward his farmhouse. "I've been in the fields since early morning. Barely seen another soul 'til you arrived."

Flatface tripped on her short legs and tumbled between the bushes, down the side of the rocky slope. Servilius pulled Cassandra back from the hillside and they clung to one another as Petronius leapt and caught the pig just at the edge of a steep ravine. It squirmed and squealed, wrenched its little body from side to side and escaped his grip. She eluded the others, darted between a pair of pine trees and disappeared.

Orestes laughed then held up his hands in despair. "There's no point in looking for her. She'll find me before I could find her."

Cassandra let out a deep sigh. "She knows who her papa is, Orestes."

"I'm sure she knows the feed trough and Orestes equally," I said. "These little runts live for their bellies."

"You know pigs, Timothy. She'll be back," said Orestes.

Servilius, oblivious to our talk, straightened and cupped her palm to her ear. "Listen," she said.

I could make out a steady rhythm ... drumming ... but crisper, like shields knocking together. "What is it?"

Orestes asked, "Do you hear singing?"

"Women's voices," Cassandra replied. "And screaming. I'm frightened. Let's go back."

The sun had dropped below the horizon and everything was turning grey.

I moved closer to Cassandra. Servilius stood between us.

"It's the fourth, isn't it?" asked Orestes. "The fourth day past April kalends?"

He didn't wait for an answer. "It's the Kybele cult. They have a spring rite. It can be gory, like your circumcision, but much worse."

He nodded in the direction of the drumming. "Come with me, Timothy. You'd like a little adventure."

"Impossible. Jesus has my allegiance. I can't insult him by joining those who worship other gods."

Cassandra shrank into the dark shadows of the trees. She peered from above the veil and gripped her shawl tightly at her shoulders.

Servilius put her arm around Cassandra and shook her head at us. "You mustn't."

Petronius stepped between us and Orestes.

A ghastly scream punctured the darkness. Petronius flinched and took a step back down the path. "Mistress, we must leave," he insisted. "I'm here to protect you. I've heard of this cult. They mutilate the flesh. We must go. Darkness has settled in. Please mistress."

We retreated. A few steps down the path, we stopped behind some thick shrubs. Through the darkness, I picked out the silhouetted figures of a procession. Some wore tall conical caps, the tips tilted forward. Several swung whips over their heads that slashed the bare skin on their backs. Others carried spears and shields. They chanted and danced, but as we watched, the frenetic pace became slower and more solemn, as if they were anticipating something. Orestes crouched like a nervous squirrel alert to danger.

"They've entered the sacred cave," he whispered, "It's below us, just out of sight."

He pulled a torch from his bag and struck a flint to light it. It encircled us with an amber glow and everything beyond it became dark and mysterious. The chanting and drumming sent a shiver down my back and raised the hairs on my neck. I felt as if the devil were very near and the torch a meager shield.

Wild screeching shattered the silence, followed by confused, clamorous shouts. Voices growled in fear and rage. Cassandra trembled and grasped my arm as another shriek pierced the night air, but this one I recognized. From the rocks below, as fast as her little legs could carry her, ran Flatface, bounding out of the darkness toward us. She leapt at Orestes and knocked him to the ground. The pig slobbered all over his tunic and face.

"Get ... off!" he cried. He pushed Flatface away. "Help. Get this swine off me."

I was too frightened to laugh, but Flatface's antics, allayed some of my fear. Petronius helped Orestes to his feet.

I scooped up Flatface and rubbed its tummy as Orestes had done. "You've got courage, little one," I said. "We froze in fear while you toddled right into their midst."

She stopped wriggling and made a piggy smile as if to say, "I'm innocent."

As we picked our way down the hill, the sounds of worship from within the sacred cave diminished and we all relaxed, feeling safe once again and giggling every few minutes as we remembered the hilarious pig.

At the bottom of the hill, Orestes stopped. "I have to see what they're doing. You can come, or take the torch and go."

"You're mad, Orestes," blurted Cassandra. "What they do is unspeakable." She snatched the torch from Orestes and started along the path. "Servilia, come with me."

"Wait for me," shouted Petronius. "I'll not put myself in danger for you, Timothy. If you're going with Orestes, be careful. Give me that stupid pig. You can't take it in the cave. They'll roast it on their ritual fire."

Petronius took Flatface and hurried away with the women.

Cassandra held the torch straight in front of her as the three of them picked their way back along the rocky path, leaving Orestes and me in darkness.

They were gone so quickly, I didn't have time to speak. Should I run after them and leave Orestes to watch the ritual with no one to help him understand the truth? Could I let Cassandra walk into the dark night after promising to keep her from harm? I gaped at Orestes.

"You don't have to come, Timothy," Orestes said. "I know these hills and can find my way by moonlight. I'll be silent as a fox."

"Orestes, reason tells me to leave these people to their perverted practices, but I won't leave you. God forgive me. I'll come, but be very careful."

I held tight to Orestes' cloak as he led the way around the hill to the devotees' path. I felt my every step betrayed Jesus, but I knew I ought to stay with Orestes for his protection. I prayed for God to be with us and hoped for the best.

Soon, my eyes adjusted to the darkness and I could see well enough to let go of Orestes. The two of us picked our way toward the cave's entrance. As we came near, we heard low murmurs invoking the names of Kybele, Mother of gods. Flutes accompanied the chants. The drums were silent. The voices slowed and then stopped as we reached the mouth of the cave, its flank illuminated by the torches inside.

Orestes grabbed my arm, pulled me to the wall and pointed to the stone above the entrance. There was a carved image of a goddess enthroned between lions. She wore a long, belted dress with a high cylindrical hat and a thin veil that covered her body. Kybele was brought to life by the fire-light flickering off her features. It made her delicate robes flow and the lions' muscles ripple with vicious power.

We sidled past the goddess and stood with the last of the worshippers. I pulled my tunic's hood over my head like the others.

At the front of the procession stood the priestesses, large Amazons, wearing bright dresses and heavy jewelry on their wrists and necks. Smaller women flanked them, dressed in vivid robes. They danced and tossed the hair of their ivy-crowned heads. One priestess climbed to a rock ledge and raised a large urn. She tipped it to her lips and poured rich, red wine into her mouth, spilling the excess over her gown and onto the earth at her feet. The crowd roared their approval and she raised her hands again. A large knife blade caught the torchlight. The drummers began a slow beat, getting faster and louder.

A young man in a loincloth staggered toward the priestess. Long hair covered his bare shoulders. His eyes stared ahead and his mouth sagged open in a lifeless face. He lay down on a stone table. Four assistants stepped forward, took off his loincloth and pinned him, spread-eagled against the table.

I turned to Orestes and mouthed the words, "What's happening?"

Orestes, eyes aflame, hissed, "Cas-tra-tio." He held his palm toward me and touched a finger to his lips to indicate silence.

I saw the knife flash as the priestess plunged its blade down. The supplicant screamed. Blood spurted into the air. Assistants immediately pressed an iron from the altar flame against his wound. They bound him with a tight undergarment. The acrid stench of burnt flesh reached us as attendants pulled him to his feet and draped a woman's sky-blue gown over him. They tied and greased his long, loose hair to match the other priestesses. They put a wine-urn in his hands. Drenched in sweat, his lips and cheeks quivered with pain. Orestes stared, not moving a muscle, not even to blink.

The transformation was complete. The eunuch priestess took the urn and held it above his head, arms shaking. In a burst of ecstasy and pain, he screamed, tipped the urn to his mouth and gulped great drafts of wine. Drum-beats exploded and cries of "Mother of Earth, Mother of gods" filled the cave. The worshippers beat spears and shields together and danced, singing and shouting.

Eyes glazed, Orestes walked toward the devotees and their rapturous dance. I grabbed him and pulled him out of the cave. We crept past the idol and found refuge behind a large rock. The worshippers were so engrossed in their ritual that no one seemed to notice our retreat.

Orestes sat back against the massive stone. His eyes stared straight ahead. I slapped him across the face. "Orestes, Orestes, wake up," I whispered. "Oh God, in Jesus' name, wake up!"

At the name of Jesus, Orestes shook his head, his eyes brightened, and he looked around. "Where am I?" he asked. "What's happening?"

His head turned toward the din from the cave. He grabbed me. "We have to go," he said.

I pulled him to his feet. "Yes. Cassandra's waiting. Hurry."

We stumbled up the hill through the black. Wispy clouds caught moon-glow and scattered a dim light along the path to Orestes' farmhouse. I took him by the arm. "What happened to you back there? I thought you were about to join their insane worship."

He pulled away from me. "I wouldn't do that. Those people are bewitched."

"But if I hadn't taken you outside you would have joined them."

His eyes looked hollow and fearful in the pale moonlight. "What are you saying? What happened?"

"You were in a trance. I slapped you to break the spell, but you only came out of it when I called the name of Jesus. His power saved you. What do you remember?"

"Heat from the crowd, dancing, torchlight, drums. Voices calling out the goddess' name over and over."

Orestes pressed his hand to his forehead. "I don't remember trying to join them. Was I spellbound, like a moth by a flame?"

"There's evil in this." I said. "Couldn't you feel it? Their ritual nearly trapped you."

Orestes looked away into the dark. At the farm gate, the light from the torch flickered, a beacon for us. When he turned back to me, his eyes were wide and his mouth sagged open. "They butchered that man, Timothy. They carved away his manhood. Barbarians!

It's not the Greek way. Some force drew me to their worship, but reason warns me against it."

"Reason serves you well. Follow a path based on a sound mind, not enchantment. Orestes, you've given your heart to God. Don't give your mind and spirit to false gods."

He shook his head. "How do you know they're false? What happened in that cave was real."

"I don't mean they're not real. I mean that they're not the true god.

If you want to follow Jesus, learn from him. He won't put you under a spell. You'll find truth in the messiah."

A turn in the path opened up the view toward Iconium. Just above the dark walls, we could see Perseus' giant head lit by torches in the open square.

Orestes pointed at the icon. "It's all so confusing. So many gods. I want the truth, but part of me was gripped by Kybele."

"That's your body's craving. The flesh dies. Jesus tells us to control our appetites and nourish the Spirit that lives forever."

"Timothy, you were circumcised to please God. How does that differ from the Kybele ritual?"

"When Paul circumcised me, he said that it can't make me right with God. Only Jesus can do that."

"Nonsense." Orestes sniffed. "Why would Paul circumcise you if it wasn't necessary? But, I don't know Judaism."

We were close to the circle of torchlight from the farm gate. I saw Petronius and Servilia pleading with Cassandra. "Later, I'll teach you more," I said. "We have to get Cassandra home safely."

As soon as Cassandra saw us, she took a quick step forward and called out, "Timothy, thank God you're all right. What happened?"

She'd pulled her scarf over her head and the pale blue silk caressed the soft flesh under her chin. Deep furrows lay between her dark, searching eyes.

Servilia tugged at Cassandra's tunic, a discreet reminder of proper decorum. It looked to me that Cassandra wanted to hug us both, her relief was so visible.

Petronius shook his head at me. "You've overstepped your bounds, young Timothy. We're trembling in fear for your safety, and ours."

"I'll explain everything," I said, and turned to Cassandra. "But first we take you home."

"Orestes, come with us" I said. "Paul is going to speak about the Cult of Kybele. He'll help you understand."

He turned toward his house. "Let me get some food."

"Not necessary," Cassandra said. "There'll be plenty left from dinner."

"Then, let's move," I said. "This night air pierces right to the bones."

I took the torch and led the way. We were alone beneath the vast canopy of stars, and my eyes searched to keep to the dirt path.

Petronius' quavering voice pierced the darkness. "Are we in danger, Timothy? Will they pursue us?"

"We were like phantoms, Petronius, hiding among them."

Cassandra whispered, "Was it ghastly? We heard screams from the trail. I was afraid for you?"

"They shed blood. A young man was initiated as a eunuch priestess."

"It was terrible," Orestes said. "They were entranced. Their ways are madness."

We neared the city gates, closed for the night.

"What's this then?" a guard shouted. "It's late. Explain yourselves."

"I'm the daughter of Julian, Praetor Maximus' clerk," Cassandra said. "We were delayed by Kybele worshippers in the hills. On my father's authority, let us through."

The guards opened the small night door and we shuffled in. Torches lit the gateway courtyard and all the main streets. Orestes face was gaunt, scratched and dust-smeared. I must have looked the same. Shrubs and pine branches had swiped my face as we'd climbed the hill and floundered along the dark paths.

Cassandra appeared untarnished by the adventure, though she looked at me with a brooding frown.

"The chants and the whips frightened me," she said. "I've heard that people carry their worship to brutal lengths and what you've told us frightens me more. What drives them so? Why do they spoil what God meant to be good and pure?"

We hurried across the street toward Julian's house. "Paul will answer those questions. I hear him preaching already."

Cassandra took us into the kitchen through a side door. The fire in the barrel-shaped clay oven cast its warm glow over the table, which was covered with platters of cooked thrush, asparagus, pastry, fruits and nuts. We ate the remains of the meal and listened to Paul's strong, intent voice.

13

Shock

"I'M SHOCKED, MY FRIENDS, THAT SOME OF YOU BELIEVE YOU MUST CUT your flesh to be accepted by the Almighty. The way to God is through his son. I'm a Jew. I thought that if I obeyed the law, made sacrificial offerings and attended synagogue, then perhaps, I would be acceptable to God. I persecuted Christians because they contradicted our forefathers' teachings."

I moved into the garden to see Paul as he told his story. He stood on a low wall, easily visible above the crowd. His beard was freshly trimmed and the bald part of his head glistened in the torchlight. He wore a white toga and I thought it gave him an air of distinction. If he were speaking in the market, I would stop to listen. He raised his hands and his face brightened.

"In Damascus, I rode with temple guards to arrest Jesus' followers. I was thrown from my mount by a flash of brilliant light and my head struck the rocky road. I pressed my hands against my ears to stop the pain, but nothing could stop the voice. 'Saul,' it said, 'why do you persecute me?'"

He held his hand to his ears and closed his eyes, acting out his tale. "I opened my eyes to see who was speaking but was blinded by a light like a thousand suns. 'Who are you, Lord?'" I asked. "From the radiance came the words, 'I am Jesus, whom you persecuted.' Then I knew the purity of the holy one. On that road, in the dust and heat, I threw myself on his mercy."

Paul lowered his hands and his voice. I strained to hear.

"It's the only way. 'Blessed are those who see their spiritual poverty,' Jesus taught, 'for theirs is the kingdom of heaven.'"

Paul called, "The messiah is like that. No matter how hard you try, you can't enter the gates of heaven without him. Not by circumcision. Not by sacrificial offerings. Not by good deeds. Only by yielding. Only the humble soul can experience his love."

Paul closed the meeting and came to me. He took my arm and we went with Silas and Julian to the atrium. I pulled my tunic tighter as we entered the room with its open ceiling and the still pool in its midst.

"Timothy," Paul asked, "how did it go with Orestes?"

"Orestes doesn't understand the difference between Judean circumcision and the Kybele rite of castration. He thinks they both show the depth of one's commitment to his god. My circumcision convinces him he's right."

"How did he get this notion?" Paul asked.

"Tonight we watched the Kybele castration rite."

Silas quickly raised his arms in prayer and paced around the room. Julian buried his face in his hands and whispered, "Cassandra?" He stared at me for a moment then rushed to the kitchen.

Paul sat heavily on a marble ledge. "Timothy, what are you saying? Did Orestes worship Kybele?"

Silas stood beside Paul. "Surely not. Tell us, Timothy."

"Yes ... I mean no. No, he didn't, but we were there. What have I done?"

Julian and Macaria rushed in with Cassandra. Macaria led her by one hand and held the other to her face.

Julian strode over and stood directly in front of me. He cleared his throat. He began carefully, but his voice rose with each word he spoke. "You've exposed our daughter to pagan religion. People may think we support Kybele. Our allegiance to Jesus may be questioned.

And you abandoned our daughter! I trusted you with her safety. I permitted far more freedom because of your connection with Paul. Explain yourself!"

I caught Cassandra's eye, hoping she'd say something. All I saw were tears and hurt. She buried her face in her mother's shoulder and wept. Macaria stared at me with venom in her eyes.

It was the worst moment of my life, and the longest.

Finally, through her tears, Cassandra said, "It wasn't his fault. Tell them, Timothy. It wasn't your fault."

Paul, still seated, called for our attention. His arms were crossed and he looked at the floor. "We'll be the judges, my dear, but first we must know the truth."

He looked up, calmly stroking his goatee with one hand. "Timothy, tell us what happened. If this is simply a matter of immaturity, we'll stand together. Don't worsen it with excuses or half-truths."

A cold breeze whistled through the atrium. Torches and candles flickered and some were snuffed by the wind. "Orestes took us for a walk and we were surprised by a procession of Kybele worshippers. We turned back to the farm as soon as we could without attracting attention but Orestes wanted to see what they were doing. He was determined and would have gone alone, so I went with him for his safety. The others went back to the farm."

I looked at Macaria. Her lips pursed in a tight line. She stared at me out of dark, narrow eyes.

"I'm sorry," I said. "I thought I was doing the best I could. Cassandra was never in danger. She was never near any of the cult's practices."

Macaria looked sideways at me. I knew she didn't accept my excuse.

"What else can I do to fix this?" I asked.

"The servants will talk," Macaria whispered to Julian. "The whole city will know before the night is over. Servilia and the rest, they're all notorious gossips."

"My dear, you must speak to them tonight," Julian urged. "Perhaps we can keep this from spreading beyond our household. We can't have people thinking we support the cult."

"Go now, Macaria," Silas said. "Take Cassandra so she can verify the truth."

"Very good," Paul said. "We must do what we can to lessen the damage."

He stood and motioned for me to take his seat. He put one foot up on the ledge and placed a hand on my shoulder. "I said that you're young and must learn responsibility. Don't let your youth keep you from doing what's right. Tonight, you yielded to Orestes' leadership when it was he who needed someone to follow. You must assert yourself."

Paul's words made me feel even worse. Not only had I failed Cassandra and betrayed Jesus, I lacked strength of character. My shoulders slumped under the weight of his hand and mercifully, he withdrew and sat beside me before continuing.

"Julian and I both trusted you to be in charge tonight. You behaved like a sheep with no shepherd. Orestes will expect the same of you the next time you meet. You've lost the crucial moment to lead him in faith."

Paul was right. I had given in to Orestes. "What can I do? I want to learn."

Paul rubbed his bald head, like a seer polishing his glass. Would he send me back to Lystra? Had I failed so badly? I wanted desperately to stay with him.

"Our presence here will only be a distraction to both gentile and Judean Christians. We will leave tomorrow."

"Julian," Paul said, "you're a mature leader. The church will thrive under you without us."

Julian shrugged and lifted an eyebrow. "Much as I want you to stay, your words are wise. Those who would destroy our reputation, the same ones who forced you from Iconium before, will have little reason to trouble us if you're not here."

Silas nodded. "Tomorrow then. I'll start packing at first light."

"Now, Timothy," Paul said. His voice was kinder and the tightness around his eyes had eased. "You'll have further assignments in the days to come, and you'll succeed. You'll grow as a leader."

"How do you know?"

"Because I've seen in you a learning heart and because God has chosen you to be with us. You can't fail in his strength."

Paul's decision was final, but I couldn't believe that our work at Iconium was complete. Was it really time to leave Cassandra? I felt hope flee my heart, and despair rush in. I managed to say goodnight, quietly find my way to my bed and snuggle into its warmth where I lay, alone with my thoughts and prayers.

Visions of the ghastly ritual kept me awake much of the night. I saw a blood-red cloud even when I closed my eyes. The smell of burning grass from torches and musty stone filled my nostrils. Voices whispered persistently in my head, 'cut, maimed and neutered. The plight of the priestess of Kybele, cut maimed and neutered.' It repeated like drumbeats until morning light.

I awoke facing the wall, its dull ochre paint inches from my face, boxed in like a caged fowl. I threw off the blanket and pulled on my tunic. I covered my face and shook my head to cast off the offensive images. Then I opened my eyes.

Cassandra sat at the atrium pool, trailing one hand in the sparkling water. She turned toward me with an uncertain smile. Her hair was piled on top of her head, baring her slender neck. I steadied myself against the door frame. She glanced at the space beside her. I wondered if I should I sit with her. Would it make things worse?

She lifted her hand from the water and beckoned me to her.

I sat beside her and dangled my feet in the cool, refreshing pool. She held my hand and leaned her head against my shoulder. Her touch surprised me. Only lovers shared such a caress.

"You mustn't, Cassandra. You're promised to someone." I placed her hand in her lap and moved away.

She pursed her lips and looked down. "It's only a promise. It was made nearly two years ago when I was a girl. It will lose its hold on me if it's not consummated with marriage soon."

She slowly raised her eyes and spoke so softly I barely heard her, "Or if I join with another."

She began tracing the pattern in the tile with one slender finger while my heart raced. I imagined the joy of living with her, but my commitment to follow Jesus and travel with Paul was sacred. Could a promise to Jehovah be broken for love? No, I thought. But, in time, God could make the two into one, if he willed it.

I placed my hand over hers and lifted it away from the tiles. "Cassandra, I love you, but my promise is to follow Jesus with Paul. We can't marry now, but we can love. Then we have to trust God to make things work for our pleasure as well as for his glory."

Cassandra shook her head. "I can't wait. I can't trust."

She looked at me, tears forming in her eyes. "Perhaps I can hope."

Voices came from the rooms above. I let go of her hand and stood. "Then I'll hope with you, that you'll soon be free from your betrothal. Be patient. There'll be joy in seeing how Jesus brings us together."

Cassandra stood and as she turned away, she allowed her hand to brush my leg. At the stairway to the women's rooms above, she paused on the bottom step. She turned and smiled at me, then hurried up the stairs.

My heart pounded and the Spirit's inner voice whispered, "She'll be yours one day, but for now, you're mine alone."

I sat by the pool for a moment longer and splashed water on my face. I'd been brave and said what I knew was true and right. I wanted to believe the inner voice, but I was torn between the joy of knowing she loved me and the heartbreak of not knowing when we might be together again.

I'd started toward my room when Paul called from his cubicle across the atrium, "Timothy, we leave for Antioch this morning. Get the cart and mule ready."

Maybe I had one last chance. "I can't undo what happened last night, Paul, but shouldn't we stay to strengthen the teaching here?"

Paul crossed the atrium courtyard and put his hand on my shoulder. His eyes were framed with dark shadows and his beard scruffy, but he smiled and spoke with certainty. "The Spirit tells me our work is done here, my son. Silas and I spoke for hours with Julian last night. We leave him solid teaching that will build up the believers. They'll know that no ritual has the power to appease God. Only Jesus' death can do that."

"And Orestes? I didn't see him all last night. How will he learn this truth?"

"I've instructed Julian to meet with Orestes and teach him every day. The way of the Nazarene will convince him. It has that power. He'll learn that faith in the chosen one is God's only requirement."

My arm fell listlessly to my side. "Then there's nothing more to say. It seems like such a short time we've been here."

"Cassandra will not easily leave your heart," Paul said.

His face wore a strange half smile.

"As you know, Timothy, Julian is highly respected in Iconium. Cassandra is promised to Appion, son of a high ranking Roman official. Appion is extremely nervous about the Jewish community who don't tolerate followers of Jesus. He won't let the betrothal proceed unless there's peace between the two factions. He also won't release Julian from the betrothal promise. So Cassandra, though promised, can't marry."

"Yet, she teases me with her friendliness," I said.

Paul rolled his eyes. "Julian says she feels free to make what friendships she wishes without regard to marriage, since that's out of the question for the time being. She's making quite a stir. Julian finds it amusing, but Macaria is distraught. Such behaviour would not be tolerated in Rome, or Jerusalem, but in this polyglot city of Iconium, there's greater latitude. God only knows what he has in store for Cassandra. She must learn her place, and find her place in the master's service"

Paul gripped my hand and stared into my eyes. "Young Timothy," he said, "your strengths are more powerful than your weaknesses. Don't let yesterday's failure shrink your resolve. I won't give up on you."

"And I won't let you down. Not ever."

He dropped my hand. "We have long journeys ahead, many cities like this where no one's heard the good news. Get things ready. We'll leave after we've eaten.

Julian and Macaria were civil as we ate that morning. I said little and began to feel out of place. While Paul and Silas said their goodbyes, I went to the stable at the back of the house to harness our mule, Ruth. Cassandra hadn't been at breakfast, and I longed to see her. I knew she loved me and I was certain that God could bring us together again, some day.

I was nearly finished when Cassandra skipped across the hay-strewn ground and held a handful of grain to Ruth's mouth which the mule grabbed with her lips and chewed contendedly. Cassandra looked at her hands. "It slobbered on me." She wiped them on Ruth's flanks.

"Ruth does that," I said, "but only to pretty young girls who break the hearts of pretty young men who have to go on a pretty long journey."

"You named her Ruth?" She asked.

"Yes, because she goes with me wherever I go."

"Don't mock me." She giggled.

"If you weren't betrothed, I'd marry you. I'd snatch you into the wagon, take you with me and change your name to Ruth."

She climbed into the wagon and sat among the bundles that Silas had packed. She said softly, "And I wouldn't resist."

I struggled against the urge to take her into my arms. I couldn't help picture how Paul's face would look if he saw me behaving in such a way. I laughed aloud at the thought.

She pouted. "Now you're laughing at me," she said, "and on the very day you're leaving."

"No. Leaving you is nothing for me to laugh about."

Cassandra climbed out of the cart. "I have something for you." She took my hand and dropped into it the fibulae she'd worn the first time we met. The figures were frozen in gold: a ravenous cat, poised to leap at two gilded birds, objects of its desire.

"To remember me by until you return," she said.

I reached for the leather thong that hung around my neck. I took off the disk Gaius had given me and tied the thong to Cassandra's fibulae. She smiled when I kissed it and placed it around my neck.

I held the wooden disk out to her. "This was given to me by a close friend when I left Lystra. Safeguard it. I'll want it back."

I put the wooden disk in her hand. I would make another to carry with me, but this would be Cassandra's. She held it up to the sun and read the words inscribed on its face: *fides, spes, caritas.*

"Faith, hope, love," she whispered. She looked up at me with a half smile.

I reached down, turned the disc over in her hand and read the word Gaius had carved there. "*Semper* ... always.

"May God be with you, Cassandra. Pray for me, as I'll pray for you. My life is the master's, but my heart is yours." I choked as I turned, took hold of Ruth's reins and led her through the courtyard gate. I heard Cassandra's quavering voice behind me.

"God be with you, Timothy. Remember, Trust in Jehovah."

We left, not knowing when, if ever, I'd return.

I plodded with Ruth to the main street where Paul and Silas waited. Petronius accompanied us and gave Paul instructions about the journey. He left him with a purse of coins from Julian to help us on our way. We stopped to bid him farewell just before we passed through the gate.

We turned our faces toward Antioch of Pisidia, the next stop on our journey, many days from Iconium and Cassandra. Clouds gathered on the mountains northwest of the city. I pulled my cloak about me. We would travel through rainstorms that day and only God knew what after that.

PART III

ANTIOCH

Run in such a way as to get the prize. 1 Corinthians 9:24

14

Fire in the Belly

THE FIRST DROPS OF RAIN FELL AS WE CLIMBED INTO THE MOUNTAINS west of Iconium. The damp, musty smell of wet dirt was soon washed away by the heavy rain and we settled into a grim march along the Via Sebaste. Once over the mountains, the road followed river valleys as far as Philomelion where we stopped after eight weary days of travel. We left the next morning while the air was still cool and travelers were few. Silas and Paul walked ahead of the wagon while I led Ruth steadily along the cobbled road.

We soon reached the customs station between Galatia and Asia. They taxed everything that wasn't for personal use, even corpses, so we paid little, while traders paid more. Most goods were taxed at two to five percent, but on luxuries like silk, perfumes, spices and pearls, it could be as much as twenty-five percent. The best merchants would still make a profit by driving hard bargains for their wares.

A farmer in his four-wheeled wagon carried vegetables, a few animals and eggs. He paid duties on his cabbages, beets, leeks and leafy greens. The small thrushes, hare and goat were also taxed and even the eggs carried by a cursor, who held them nestled in a bundle of straw.

The farmer gripped the collar of a small black goat and pled with the official. "Sir, you mustn't tax our Kara. She's family. You wouldn't tax my son, or my daughter."

He'd barely uttered the words when Kara bucked and kicked the cursor, who flew across the road and tripped over his feet while he protected the bundle of eggs in his arms. The farmer wrestled the goat into submission and tied it to his cart frame. Kara wriggled and fussed the whole time, bleating her annoyance at the laughing travelers watching them.

"Pay the fee or forfeit the family," the agent ordered.

The farmer fumbled in his money bag and dropped the required coins into the steel-strapped Imperial box, then drove his cart hard from the custom station while his cursor ran to keep up. When he was out of earshot, the agent mumbled, "Thank the gods he paid. His wretched family's not a prize the emperor would welcome in place of the coin."

Paul and I paid tax on our tools. We were able to convince the agent that our poor mule was a beast of burden and not for sale.

We followed the Anthius River until we saw the city. Antioch perched on soft brown hills in front of snow topped mountains. It had seven districts, each on a separate hill, just as in Rome. The acropolis and marble temple of Augustus shone in the sun.

Paul said that fifty thousand people lived in Antioch, many of them crowded in multi-story apartments. Rooms in the centre had no windows and no openings for fresh air. I was a village boy used to our roomy home with rooftop sleeping pads in the summer. Antioch didn't sound appealing, in spite of the impressive Roman temple towering on the slope above us.

Inside the walls, Silas stopped the cart where a fountain splashed fresh water. We rested and drank from the pool.

"I have friends here," Paul said. "They make and sell furniture and tent cloth. Hector and Sappho were two of my first converts after I preached in the synagogue. Their son, Polites and his wife, Helvia live with them. They gave us lodging and food. Jehovah blessed their hospitality. We'll stay with them so he can bless them all the more." He laughed at his comment and slapped me on the back.

"Come Timothy, Silas. You'll meet my good friends and we'll all be in their debt. With Jesus, both asset and debt are shared, aren't they?"

Silas pulled the money bag from his tunic and turned it inside out. "For now, it's only debt we share, my friend. Lead on."

We reached the temple at the main cross street. The twelve steps and huge gateway, the Propylon, that led to the temple looked like a squadron of guards, a marble image of the Roman Empire's strength and security. The perfectly proportioned beauty, dominated the city. A short distance north of the temple, we took a narrow road west toward a crowded neighbourhood.

"My friends live just along this street," Paul said. "They'd been converts to Judaism in order to trade with Jewish merchants. When they heard of Jesus they saw the fulfillment of their quest to know God. They came every time I preached and pestered me with questions. We stayed with them until the Jewish women stirred the people up. The riot forced us out of Antioch."

We passed several large apartment buildings before coming to a two-story with a spacious shop on the ground floor. Through the doorway, I saw furniture, rugs, vases and, in one corner, goat hair cloth for tents.

Silas stayed with the cart while Paul and I went into the taberna. It smelled of oiled wood and bleached wool. A table holding carved wooden bowls stood just inside the entrance and as I examined them, a tall, lean man with short dark hair stepped through a curtain at the back.

"Polites!" Paul shouted. They embraced and Paul turned to me. "This is Timothy. Our companion, Silas, is outside with the cart. We just arrived from Iconium."

Polites took my hand and hugged me. "My friends, We have rooms for you. "Helvia!" he called. "Come and see. Paul's back."

"Paul!" we heard from behind the curtain.

A tiny robust woman strode into the room. Her hair, the color of autumn leaves, hung in two braids over her shoulders. She threw her arms around Paul's waist. "I knew you'd be back. You still haven't tasted my lamb pie. Those riotous women forced you out of the city the very night I'd baked it. Bless God. I have one in the oven now. We'll feast your return."

She hugged him again, turned and grabbed me around the waist. "My, you're tall. The birds must be your friends," she said. "Now, husband, get them settled. We'll eat as soon as the dark drives Hector and Sappho home from the market."

Polites showed us to rooms in the back where we'd sleep. There was space for our mule and cart just off the small path beside the shop. I unloaded the packs and settled Ruth for the night. Paul and Silas had gone indoors to get warm. That day we'd seen the mountains north of Antioch coated in snow, beautiful in the sunshine. But when the sun went down, it got cold very quickly.

Polites asked if I needed any help.

"But you're needed in the shop," I said.

"We've closed. Always at nightfall. How was your journey?"

"Good. We left Iconium ten days ago and have had no delays. Lots of travelers at first, going west to Ephesus in spite of the danger."

Polites shrugged. "Roman patrols don't seem to stop the brigands. Only ten days from Iconium with a mule and cart is good travelling. Couriers can do it in a little more than a day, but they have fresh horses and riders at the posting stations."

"Just over a day! I can't believe it."

"Oh yes," Polites said, "though the Imperial Post takes about four days. I've run the route in five, travelling very light and alone.

"Five days!" Again, I was astounded. "How could you do it? You're mocking me."

"No, no Timothy. I used to train for the Olympics. I once placed second to the regional champion in the dolichos, but couldn't afford to go on to Olympus to compete. It was my best finish and I never had the opportunity again. Now I help train our younger athletes at the stadium. The regional eliminations begin next month. Maybe you'll have time to go with me while you're here."

"I never had much time for the games," I said, "except when I was a child. We'd each take the name of a great champion like Leonidas of Rhodes, and run as if we were him. We had no trainers in Lystra, so I never competed."

"I could train you and see how you do."

"Too late for me, Polites. I'm committed to serving the master with Paul, but I'd like to go to the stadium with you."

"Well then, consider it done."

Polities gripped my shoulders and looked me over. We were about the same height and build. "You have a distance runner's long legs and lean body. You should run with my boys tomorrow. But now, it's time to meet my parents don't you think?"

The kitchen was a large room with expansive counters, a large oven and a fireplace. Cooking implements hung from a rack over the counter. The room was packed with people, all talking at once. Before Polites could introduce me, his mother, Sappho, a rotund woman, with a hint of mischief in her eyes, interrupted all conversation.

"Talk, talk, talk! Keep this up any longer and we'll never get the meal ready. Hector, take our guests into the house-place so we can get to work. Why you insist on entertaining in my workspace, I'll never understand."

Hector placed both large fists on his wide hips. "Sappho, my darling, this is my favourite room because it contains the two loves of my life, you, my dear, and your wonderful food ... or perhaps it's the other way around, the food first and you second."

Sappho shook her broom at Hector.

"All right, all right, I'm leaving. Put up your broom."

We all laughed.

Their actions struck me to the core and I felt the lack of my deepest need. I touched Cassandra's fibulae at my neck. I railed against her betrothal to Appion. Why wouldn't I accept the truth? I longed to marry her, to have her by my side whatever life brought. Was it just a dream, never to be realized? By the time I shook myself out of these thoughts, Hector was speaking.

"Here, in our houseplace, we eat, work and talk. Please, sit and make youselves busy. While the women cook, we'll work. It's our way."

Weaving and carpentry tools hung on the walls like works of art and the stone tiled floor and brick walls glowed from oil lamps in the wall niches. Rough, unfinished wooden bowls nested in stacks by the walls.

"Those will be for trade and for sale," Hector said. "Knives and chisels are on the wall. Let's begin."

Polites showed us where to sit and gave us knives to carve the wood into bowls. I helped Silas who was a quick learner. Paul found his way to a spindle and distaff in one corner and began spinning from a pile of black goat hair.

"Tomorrow," Polites said, "I'll take the three of you to the stadium. You'll meet my athletes. Their education is in my hands and I want you to speak to them. There's more to running than healthy bodies and fast legs. Courage, drive, fire in the belly..., men with a powerful inner spirit excel. You give them that, my friends, and my runners will become winners."

15

Let the Games Begin

POLITES TOOK US TO THE STADIUM EARLY THE NEXT DAY. WE WALKED with throngs of people along the Cardo Maximus, past the busy shops and street merchants. Paul stopped when we reached the brick entrance to the synagogue. He pointed his staff at the arched doorway. "King David's words when he was in exile and longed for the temples are inscribed on the floor in there:

"These things I remember as I pour out my soul:
how I used to go with the multitude,
leading the procession to the house of God,
with shouts of joy and thanksgiving
among the festive throng..."

Paul's voice broke and he leaned on his staff.

"I'm crushed, as David was," he cried. "Here, I once preached and was welcomed. The leaders saw the great crowds that came to hear my teaching and shut the doors to me. I long for its familiar walls, for the scrolls and the lively debates."

He fell to his knees. He placed his hands on the tiled courtyard and choked out a prayer, "God of Israel, Father of all who follow Jesus, fulfill your purpose in this structure of wood and brick. Make it a place where your Son is worshipped and all who love him will be welcomed."

Silas knelt beside him. "Be calm, my friend. I know your heart loves Israel and your people. Have faith. Remember Hector, Sappho and Polites. God is at work in this city."

"Come, Paul," Polites said. "It's not safe for us to stay. The Judean's keep watch. They'll stone you and drive you out again."

Paul struggled to his feet. "Yes, bless you, my son," he said. "We must go. Our work is in the houses of those who love Jesus, like yours. Lead on."

Polites took us further along the street and pointed beyond the walls to a well-worn, marble stadium. "There's the very place to work your body to its finest. It's an old structure, but with a full track of 540 feet, one *stade*. The length was set by Herakles – the distance he ran in one breath before taking another. We run the *stade* twenty-four times in the *dolichos* race."

"I can run that distance," I said, "but I'd need at least two breaths."

Polites laughed as we passed through the city gate where an army of men were working a construction site.

"What's all this?" I asked.

"That's been in the works my whole life. They're building an aqueduct to bring unlimited fresh water from the mountains. Next to it, a center for athletic training and contests. Baths, a *palaestra* for wrestling. A *nymphaeum* between as a monument to the spring nymphs."

We hiked up the eastern side of the stadium and sat near the judges stand. From there, the valley fell to the north and in the distance loomed the towering, snow-covered mountains.

"My athletes swear an oath to train hard for the games in August," Polites said. "Then they travel to Elis, in Greece, for the final stage. I train my boys hard, but few have the wealth it takes to travel and spend a month at Elis before the games."

As Polites finished speaking, six young men entered the stadium and he stood to face them.

"Polites," they said, "we salute you. We are at your service."

"So be it," Polites said. "Begin with the usual warm ups, then five lengths of the stadium at three quarter speed. Meet me here when done. Go!"

He turned to us. "Those are my protegees: Claudius, Clytheris, Priam, Jason, Pallas and Phillip. Only Clytheris qualified last year, but they've formed a pact to push each other harder. Clytheris and Phillip have the best chance. They're the oldest to compete as boys. All but Priam will compete as men at the next Olympics in four years. Timothy, you must join them."

"Join them? Me? Polites, I can't compete against trained athletes. I'd make a fool of myself."

"Don't think that. These boys are here to train, not to humiliate one another. I'll introduce you as a friend, here for a day of training. It'll give you a chance to know them and tell your story of faith. Don't worry, they're under my instruction and will treat you with respect. What do you say?"

"Well, I can't say no to that. Polites, I salute you. I'm at your service."

"Paul," I asked, "can you manage without me for the morning?"

Paul wore a sly look, as though suffering fools gladly but his response was patient. "Timothy, my son, If I could run even one stade and was young as you, I wouldn't pass up such an opportunity, particularly if it lets you to spread the good news."

He turned to Polites. "Don't leave it to chance, Polites. Exercise their spirits as well as their bodies. You know how the crowds love a champion."

"Paul, you have my word. Their parents expect them to be well educated when we're done with them. Timothy will teach his faith as part of their education."

"Well then, Silas and I will watch."

We trotted side by side to the track. "When I was young," he said, "I wanted to compete in all three Olympic footraces: The *dromos*, one stadium length; the *diaulos*, a race around the *kampter*, or turning post, and back; and the *dolichos*, twelve times to the *kampter* and back, nearly three miles. I trained for all three, like the great Leonidas. Four times he won all the races including the *hoplitodromos*: a *diaulos*, run wearing a helmet and shield.

"I always thought it possible to win the short races as well as the dolichos, but could never do it," said Polites. "I've been working on some techniques that may make it possible one day. Clytheris and Phillip, maybe. They'd make me proud.

"As for you, Timothy, you've been on the road for ten days. Do you have any pains or cramps?"

"After the first two days, I had no trouble. I got impatient with our progress, but our mule has one speed: slow. Sometimes I run ahead and wait for the others to catch up. I'll enjoy the freedom to run today."

"Good, then do some stretching and warm up with two *diaulos*."

The sun was full and bright, the morning's sharp cold gone. I stretched and ran to the *kampter* and back. When I stripped to my waistcloth and went back onto the track for a few more laps, the other runners were there. I fell in step with them and we exchanged names. Pallas and Phillip were locals, the others from various cities and towns throughout Galatia. We did two more laps of the stadium before Polites called us to him.

"Well done, young men. That's enough warm-up. You've met my friend, Timothy? He's joining us for the morning. He arrived yesterday from Iconium and wants to stretch his legs. He'll tell you about himself after we've done our first hour's training."

We practiced race starts to get used to the *hysplex*, a starting gate held up by cords. When the cords were dropped, the gate fell to the ground. I learned to take a little leap to avoid tripping over the gate.

Just before midday, Polites announced that we'd do a half *dolichos*, six laps of the track.

"Remember," he said, "don't touch the *kampter*, not even to steady yourself on the turn. After the race, we'll talk about distance-running strategy. First, run the race your way. It will give you something to compare in our discussion later."

I decided I'd just try to keep up with the others. We all got off the marks cleanly and I saw that Claudius and Pallas started fast, almost at the speed of a Diaulos. Before I knew it, I was the last runner.

I was determined to at least finish. By the second turn, I was half a length behind, but the leaders were already tiring and the others were closing on them. By the fourth turn Claudius dropped out, gasping for breath and Pallas had slowed so much, I passed him. I was in fifth place with two more laps. I increased my pace. The gap between me and the others decreased as we approached the fifth turn. I caught Priam and Jason, but Phillip and Clytheris were well ahead.

As I rounded the *kampter* for the final length, I heard Paul and Silas cheering from the stands. It broke my concentration and I almost tripped, but caught myself. With the last of my strength I made it to the finish, just three strides behind Phillip, but a good eight behind Clytheris.

I couldn't breathe. I doubled over. My legs gave out and I fell to my knees. The stadium faded from view. Phillip grabbed me around the shoulders and hoisted me to my feet.

"Walk it off," he said. "You have to keep moving."

We hobbled along the track until I had enough breath to talk. "I've never been so exhausted," I wheezed. "I almost passed out. How can you do this for twelve laps?"

Phillip looked like he was still running. He bounced up and down on his feet. His fair hair waved like a swelling sea. "Timothy, this is my specialty," he said. "I always run the *dolichos*. Claudius and Pallas are *dromos* runners. This is the first time they've run more than a *diaulos*. It all depends what you train for."

My legs felt like a new born lamb's as I staggered to the judges' stand where everyone was gathering, including Paul and Silas.

"Well done, Timothy," Paul said. "You gave it your all, as if you were running for a prize."

"No prize, Paul. Just a training run. I don't know why I ran so hard."

"I do," said Polites. "You love to race. A runner is either champion, or loser. Only one gets the prize. Some run aimlessly, their fists pumping the air and their lungs sucking impotently, running the wrong race in the wrong way."

He turned to his athletes. "Now, who felt that way? Claudius, yes. When did you feel you were running the wrong race?"

"I knew it at the first turn. I knew I couldn't keep up the pace for twelve lengths, but I had to keep in front. I couldn't even finish. I'm ashamed," Claudius said.

"Don't be," said Polites. "You're a good runner. You'll win many *dromos*, but you need training for the *dolichos*.

" Pallas, what about you? You finished last but for Claudius. What happened?"

"I had no breath after the third turn. I had to slow down, but I recovered near the end. Did you see I was running faster then?"

"I did," said Polites. "I'll watch you, maybe train you for the *dolichos*.

"Now, Timothy, what did you learn from this run? It looked like you were in trouble from the start, yet you finished third."

"When I saw Claudius and Pallas start out fast, I knew I could never match them, so I settled into a pace that felt comfortable without getting too far behind. When the others tried to catch up to the leaders, I also tried, but I didn't have the training for it. When the leaders slowed, I realized I was still in it. It was an advantage to be last. From there I could change my plan depending on what happened in front of me."

"Very good," said Polites. "Now listen, all of you. In the short races, you think only about running as fast as you can with your eye on the finish. You must finish first! In the *dolichos*, if you run without a plan, you're like a boxer beating the air. He hits nothing, tires himself out and never wins.

"Everyone who competes in the games trains hard. They punish their bodies to make themselves strong and ready. They all want to win. I've seen athletes come to the contests with great confidence because they've never lost. They lead from the start and don't think about the other competitors. Then, near the end, they're beaten from behind by a runner who's watched, paced himself and waited until the right moment to put every last ounce of energy into the finish. By the time the leader's been passed, it's too late."

Polites looked at each of us. "I'll train you how to run," he said, "but what's more important, I'll teach you how to plan your race so you win. That's enough training for this morning. Get your clothing and come back here, Timothy has a story to tell about the prize that's above all others. Quickly now!"

"Timothy!" Polites called, "Your cloak's here, I collected it while you were running. Listen," he said, lowering his voice. "You ran well, smooth and unafraid. With training, you could be a champion. Think about it. I'd be honoured to work with you."

"Polites, I'm flattered. I'll give you my answer in the story I tell."

It had turned chilly so I pulled on my tunic and wrapped my wool cloak over it. We all sat on the embankment and I thanked the runners for letting me race with them and for their sportsmanship.

"You're a dedicated team," I said. "It's hard to keep up such rigorous training. I don't know if I could do it, day after day, as you do and I know I'm not third-best among you."

"You were today," said Phillip.

"That's right," called Clytheris. "Join us."

The others shouted their agreement. Polites nodded his head and pointed at me. Silas and Paul looked at each other. What were they thinking?

I raised my hands and said, "I was third because four of you thought you could win and tired yourself out early. I knew I couldn't win, but kept my pace to the end. So today, Clytheris takes the prize. Another day, perhaps someone else. There's a prize in life, too. Few know of it. I found it two years ago and now my purpose is to tell you. For me, in spite of the thrill I feel in a good race, that crown is greater than a laurel wreath. You men have chosen a worthy goal. I wish you all great success. But I know your lives would be more fulfilled if you discovered this: 'there is a way that seems right but in the end it leads to death.' A wise man, Solomon, said that. A greater man made this powerful claim: 'I am the way, the truth and the life, no one comes to God, the Father, except through me.' Let me tell you about this man."

Phillip raised his hand toward me. "Speak on, runner," he said. "You philosophize like a true Greek. Who is this man?"

Phillip never seemed to stop moving. His heels bounced on the dirt while he sat. He smiled eagerly, clearly wanting to hear more.

"It's noble to compete," I said, "whether for self, Caesar or Jupiter. But it's a much greater thing to compete for the God of love. You worship many gods, but Jesus is the one I praise. He died to make things right between you and God, then he rose from the dead to prove that the spirit lives on. If you believe, he'll be your companion and trainer now and forever. And you'll have eternal life, the greatest prize. That's what I believe. Think about it."

"We will," Phillip said. He leaped to his feet and threw a ball to Jason.

Jason tossed it onto the field and shouted "*Harpaslum!*"

"I'm judge and scorekeeper," said Pallas. "Timothy, Claudius and Priam are one team. Clytheris, Phillip and Jason the other. Timothy's team to my right. Clytheris's to the left. You see the line marking centre. Go!"

I hadn't played *harpaslum* for years, but jumped to my feet. Pallas threw the ball up and Clytheris punched it into the air toward Phillip. Claudius tackled Clytheris, too late and they both fell to the ground. I launched myself at Phillip as soon as he got the ball and pushed him away so he couldn't get it into the air again. When it landed, I scooped it up and threw it to Priam on our side of the field, scoring a point for us. Priam punched it right back at me and I to him, so it crossed the center again, scoring another point. Then Phillip tackled me.

"Foul!" Pallas shouted. "Phillip struck Timothy while the ball was over the line. Another point for Timothy's team."

We played until we were exhausted. Our team won by three points. The game drew us together and there was a lot of good-natured kidding as they shared their food with me. I looked for Paul, Silas and Polites, but they were gone.

"It's an honour to train under Polites," Pallas said. "He's the greatest athlete ever from Antioch."

"He never reached the Olympics," said Clytheris, "but he was the city champion in all three footraces and everyone believed he could have won at Elis if he'd gone."

"Really," I said. "How good was he?"

"He lost only once in regional championships," Phillip said. "It was in the *dolichos*, but he'd already won the *dromos* and *diaulos* that morning. He almost became the only athlete in the region ever to complete the triple."

"He told me he finished second in the *dolichos*," I said, "but didn't say anything about his wins."

"He doesn't," Pallas said, "unless you ask him. I want to be like Polites. He's strong, honest, and pushes us hard. My older brother used to run against him and he didn't have anything good to say about him, but I see none of that arrogance in Polites now. He's told us his life changed when he believed in Jesus, but I don't see why religion should make any difference."

"Like you say, Pallas, religion doesn't make a difference. People worship what they will, but they don't change how they live. Jesus is different. He taught us to love one another and he showed us how to do that."

"How?" Phillip asked.

"By trusting God to look after our interests. Then we can give more attention to others' needs. It's about giving, rather than taking."

Polites walked across the field and sat with us while I carried on.

"Will you follow Jesus?" I asked.

"But if I do that, how can I compete?" asked Priam. "We have to make an oath to Jupiter."

"Why is that a problem?" asked Clytheris. "We can make the oath, that we'll do nothing to harm the games and that we won't cheat. I don't see a problem. Polites, do you?"

"I've thought of this since the day I chose to follow Jesus," Polites said. "The oath itself is true to our faith, but there are two problems. The first is whether the oath is made to Jupiter, or to the contests themselves. The second is that the oath is made over the entrails of a sacrificial boar. On the third day they sacrifice a hundred oxen to Jupiter and the athletes eat the meat. This may mean that if you choose to follow Jesus, you can't take the oath or take part in the sacrifices. You'll be disqualified before ever straining at the *hysplex*. Do you have the courage to risk that?"

"Courage. Sounds like stupidity to me," Pallas shouted. He kicked the ground beneath his feet. "I want to run. That's all that matters."

"If the games were tomorrow, what would you do, Polites?" I asked.

"It's an easy decision for me," Polites said. "My life was changed when I chose to live the way of Jesus, but my love for running has remained. I used to run to win. I ran to beat others, proving I was better, faster, stronger than everyone. It made me feel like a god. Now I run to please my master. I run because he's given me great speed. My purpose is to bring others to know Jesus. If I never compete in the contests again, so be it. God doesn't take away the gifts he gave when he created us. Each one must determine how to please God by using those talents in his service. I've chosen to do so by training athletes.

"If I were at the Olympics, I would proudly swear to do nothing to harm the contests and refrain from cheating. I would make this solemn oath to Jesus, my master, not Jupiter. From what I've been told, little is made of Jupiter at the contests these days, although he's an important symbol. Rome is tolerant of all religions and athletes come from all parts of the empire. They stand before Jupiter and swear in his name because it's no affront to their gods. Nevertheless, if I were forced to swear to Jupiter, I would not. Neither would I eat the sacrificial boar. If that brings disqualification, so be it. I must stand for Jesus. I know there is one God and I can't bow to another or swear in its name. So, my brave athletes, you have much to think about. Will you give your life to Jesus? Will you stand for the truth no matter what the consequences? I ask you to think about this tonight and we'll meet again tomorrow. Today was preparation. Tomorrow, intensity. We're going to run into the mountains. You need to learn how to pace yourself for the *dolichos*. When we finish, be ready to tell me your decision about Jesus. Don't worry, you're my athletes. I won't abandon you no matter what. Some of you, the most talented and the most disciplined, will compete and win. But will you win the contests, or will you win life? It's up to you."

Phillip, Pallas and I walked together back toward Hector's shop.

"My uncle would never let me do something that kept me from competing," Pallas said. "You're asking too much for the sake of religion."

Phillip punched him on the arm. "As long as we can make the oath, Pallas, we can compete. You worry too much."

"You don't know my uncle," Pallas said as he turned along the street toward his home.

"Timothy," Phillip said, "I love running, you know I do, and I love competing. There's nothing like finishing a race, knowing you've given all you have and done your best. When I win, it's as if I've conquered the world. When Polites declared that his faith is stronger than his dedication to the games, I knew I'd discovered something worth giving my life to. Tell me, how can I have faith like you and Polites?"

We walked side by side along the road toward Phillip's home. "It's much like having faith in Polites," I said. "You follow his instructions so you can become a champion. Do the same with Jesus. Put your life in his hands. Learn his teachings and live his way. We'll teach you, just as Polites trains you for the games."

We were in the open square near Hector's. At the taberna opposite, men were drinking and cursing in the torchlight. Phillip stepped away and faced me. He raised his arm forward, palm down. "Jesus, I salute you, I am at your service." He bowed his head, then looked at me. "Am I one with you, like Paul said?"

"You are one with us, Phillip and with Jesus. He's your coach. Now, go with God. Rest well for the run tomorrow."

He wrapped his arms around me for a second, then sprang up and down on his feet, as if in preparation for a race. A huge smile spread across his face. "Go with God I will," he said, "fast as the wind."

He ran toward a dark, narrow street next to the *taberna*. "Look, Vargas," one of the men called to a friend. "Leonidas streaks by. Say, boy, are you this fast in bed?"

They laughed and staggered into the street as they watched Phillip race down the cobbles toward home.

16

Moment of Truth

POLITES AND I TROTTED THROUGH HEAVY FOG ON SLICK STREETS THE next morning. When we reached the track, his six athletes were waiting. Pallas took my hand. "Run with us, Timothy."

He held my arm up toward Polites. All the boys did the same and stood in a circle around their coach. Phillip shouted, "Polites, we salute you, our coach and brother."

"Brother?" Polites said. "What does this mean, Phillip?"

"Your team stands for the truth of Jesus. Our oath is to him, not to Jupiter."

"When did this happen?"

"Last night. Phillip came to our houses and brought us together. He said he'd chosen to follow Jesus and convinced us to join him."

"What about your father?"

"In this I must do what I think is right," said Pallas. "I'll run faster now, because I run for a greater prize."

"Then, let's run." Polites held his hand up to the sky. "For you, Jesus!" he shouted. "To the mountains!" He led us out of the stadium toward the steep slopes beyond.

He set a quick pace and I thought we all ran faster and more easily than the day before. Now we ran as brothers, with the unselfish goal of pleasing God. The competition to beat one another had become a competition to spur one another on.

When the path got steeper and I slowed, Pallas pushed me from behind. "You can do it, Timothy. Don't quit."

Phillip ran right behind Polites shouting, "Go! Go! Never stop!"

At the crest of the hill, where the path opened up, we separated and Polites watched us while he caught his breath. "I see more spirit, more energy today. It's downhill now. Don't lose your footing."

"There they are!" came a shout from the path in front of us. Through the fog, I saw Vargas, one of the men who'd been at the *taberna* the night before. He led a group of men brandishing clubs.

"Get them!" Vargas yelled.

They ran toward us, throwing rocks and swinging their clubs. We dodged and held up our hands to fend them off.

"Steady boys!" Polites shouted. "Run!"

The attackers were older, heavier and tired from their climb. I ran toward the hillside where the path led down to Antioch. A stone glanced off my shoulder and I turned to see Vargas swing his club at Pallas. It slammed into his leg. He fell down screaming and grabbed one knee. Vargas stood over Pallas, ready to swing his weapon again.

I ran and threw myself at Vargas. He dropped his club and tumbled into a small pine tree. From behind I heard a thud.

"Phillip!" Polites shouted.

I swung around to see Phillip sprawled on the ground. Blood seeped from his ear.

"You've killed that boy!" Polites screamed. "Murderers!" He ran to Phillip.

Vargas struggled out of the pine. He saw Phillip. All his men stood and watched their leader.

Jason and Priam knelt over Phillip. Polites stood in a fighting crouch ready to attack any who came near.

"Done." Vargas croaked. He picked up his club and pointed to the path. The men disappeared into the mist.

Polites held his hand to his forehead. When he took it away, I saw blood on his head. He stumbled over to Phillip.

Pallas tried to stand, but his leg collapsed. I helped him hop over to the others.

Polites held his hand to Phillip's mouth. "He's breathing, but there's swelling and bleeding. We have to get him home."

We broke branches and strung our tunics between them. Polites, Priam, Clytheris and Jason each took one corner. We picked our way down the mountain with Phillip on the stretcher while Polites and I helped Pallas.

"This is my fault," Pallas said. "My father, Marcus Severus, is a powerful merchant. Last night I told him I'd decided to follow Jesus. He railed at me and at Paul, calls him a troublemaker. Says Paul was thrown out of the synagogue."

I said nothing. We couldn't blame Pallas for his father's hateful actions. Maybe Marcus would see his son's injury and be ashamed.

I took Pallas home. His father wasn't there and when his mother saw her son, she called a servant to help Pallas to a bed. She left me standing in the doorway. When I got to back Hector's, everyone was in the houseplace. I fell into a chair beside Silas and buried my head in my hands.

Silas put an arm around me. "Polites told us, Timothy. Your athletes have suffered so soon. We've been praying that they'd remain strong."

A red slash marked Polites forehead. I begged him to tell me about Phillip.

He touched his head. "I took him home, Timothy. He's resting, but he lies so still, as if he were dead."

"Pallas said it's all his fault. His father hates Paul. Are we safe now?"

"We'll have no peace while Paul is here," Hector said. "I know Marcus. His business is his god. He'll allow nothing to interfere."

Polites gripped Paul's wrist. "I urge you," he said. "Leave here before dawn and take the road north. They'll look for you to the west, but few travellers take the northern road, toward Mysia."

Polites is right," Hector said, "Tomorrow, Marcus Severus will stir the city up and drive you out. You're safe until then."

"But Phillip?" I cried. "Will he be all right?"

Polites put his arm on my shoulder. "Phillip breathes, but that's all. He can't talk to you."

"We must pray," Silas said. "We need the master's guidance and Phillip needs to be healed."

We prayed with more urgency than I'd ever heard. Though I'd known Polites' athletes for only a few days, their competitive spirit and their friendship had strengthened my own motivation to serve Jesus. I'd learned from them, particularly Phillip, and I was determined to do what I could. After some time I felt a touch on my shoulder. It was Paul, with Polites beside him. The three of us left, while Silas, Hector and the women prayed.

Night fell as we walked through the streets. "We'll go to Phillip," Paul said. "And pray the Lord will bring him back to life and strength."

Polites led us to Phillip's home and tapped on the door. A woman opened it.

"Polites," she said. "You bring these men to my home while my husband is away?"

"Clodia, they're here to help. Timothy is Phillip's friend and Paul has the Spirit of God in him. He can heal Phillip."

Her tear-stained eyes brightened, but a shadow crossed her face. "The streets are dangerous! Come in, quickly." We got in and shut the door. "Some will riot for any cause, so they can loot and pillage."

She looked at Paul. "Sir, please, if you can help my son, do it now."

"I can't heal Phillip," Paul said as he approached the pallet where Phillip lay. "Only the Lord God of heaven can."

Paul put his hand on Phillip's brow, then on his chest. "He's breathing," Paul said, "Very shallow, but he's alive." Paul knelt, one hand raised to heaven and the other on Phillip's head. He closed his eyes and prayed, "Father, here is one of your new-born followers. Restore life to him. Heal the wounds he suffered for you and raise him from this bed to serve you. In the name of your Son, Jesus, so be it."

Polites and I stood silently, waiting for some sound or motion from Phillip. I held my breath. Phillip groaned, opened his eyes, and groaned again.

Clodia gasped and rushed to his side. "Oh, Phillip, my son! Speak to me."

Phillip shut his eyes. Deep furrows lined his brow. When he opened them and looked at his mother, he whispered, "Mother... Oh, my head. What happened?"

"You were clubbed in the head, Phillip," Paul said. "Now rest. It'll take time for your strength to return and the pain to subside. We thought you might not survive, but thank God, you're back."

Paul turned to me. "Timothy, sit with Phillip. Make sure he rests while I talk to his mother. Here's some myrrh resin. Have him chew a little to ease the pain."

"Here, Phillip. Take this," I said, and held a piece of the resin to his mouth. His eyes shifted as he looked at me but he took the resin and began chewing.

"You've proven your leadership today, my friend, my courageous friend," I said. "Every one of the boys stood up for Jesus because of your conviction. You've got to get strong again and set the pace. They need you."

He lifted his head weekly, but it dropped to the pillow and he whispered, "God is my strength." He held his hands to his temple with his eyes squeezed shut. He chewed the resin until his face relaxed. He dropped his hands to his side and slept.

We slipped away and reached the safety of Polites' home. Paul called us together and reported the night's events. "I know we've stirred up the city," he said. "Messiah's truth does that. It offends the Jew and confuses the Greek, but we must make it known."

He turned to me. "You showed great courage, Timothy. You didn't compromise or shy away. You taught the truth. These athletes will change the city."

Polites put his arm around my shoulder. "Well done, my brother."

The smile and the pride I saw in his face lifted my spirit. I felt stronger and more confident than I had at Iconium, but I knew I could never let my guard down. I couldn't let myself be defeated by my weaknesses.

PART FOUR: MYSIA AND BITHYNIA

Blessed is the one who perseveres. James 1:1

17

Gods Aplenty

WE AROSE EARLY THE NEXT MORNING. POLITES LED US TO THE NORTH gate near the stadium. Silas, Paul and I would march toward the shores of the Propontis and the provinces of Mysia and Bithynia. We knew neither the people, nor their languages. How would we tell them the story of Jesus?

Just beyond the gate, ten Roman soldiers stood by the road. They watched as though they'd been waiting for us.

Their leader, a *decanus*, judging by the red floret on his helmet, stepped toward Polites.

"Polites," he barked. "You were part of the disturbance here yesterday."

"Sir, we were attacked without reason and my athletes were injured. One may never compete again. You should be hunting our assailants. I can give you their names."

"Others are investigating them. I'm Septimus. My duty is to see you safe as far as Lake Akrotiri. We've been dispatched to stop a dispute between fishermen."

"Thank you," Polites said. He pointed to us. "These three go with you, I'm staying."

"Very well." Septimus called his troop to attention, then ordered them into formation. Five soldiers marched in front of us and five behind.

We travelled northwest, crossing streams that flowed from the highlands to the lakes. Fertile valleys blossomed with chestnut trees and fields of fresh, green shoots of grain. On the mountains, scrubby oaks grew up to the snowline.

Snowdrops and crocuses dotted the meadows near mountain streams. Early one morning we saw three fallow deer grazing by a stream, always alert for tigers and leopards. He makes me to lie down in green pastures, He leads me beside still waters, he restores my soul. Not a care in the world, I thought, as we marched between the ranks of soldiers.

Fields soon gave way to wild hillsides, steep and rocky. The further we got from the city, the more rugged and desolate the landscape. At mid-day, we arrived at a meadow by a small lake. Clouds shielded us from the sun. The soldiers halted. Two stood watch and the others rested.

"We'll stop here a bit," Septimus told us. "See to your beast and gear. The next part of our journey goes past the lake and up the river valley. Tomorrow we climb a steep mountain pass. After that the road to Ipsus is easier. We can't take you all the way. As it is, we're adding a full day to our march."

I unhitched Ruth and tethered her to a stake to graze. Silas and Paul sat on the ground. Septimus, ever alert, rested against a boulder. With the experience of a well trained leader, he kept his attention on his men while he spoke to Paul.

"Further north, Gauls raid towns and travellers," Septimus said. "Antioch has authority all the way to the south shore of Akrotiri, but it's impossible to patrol all the foothills in this vast countryside. We've abandoned the remote regions, where you're going, to raiders we've never been able to tame. Stay on the Roman road."

We camped that night in a glade of cypress trees by a small creek. Septimus gave orders for the night's sentry rotation, then left his men to construct their camp and joined us at the fire we'd built. He took off his helmet. I'd thought of him only as a warrior, but when I saw the scar on his forehead and right ear, and the tiredness around his eyes, I knew his armor concealed a vulnerable man.

Septimus and his soldiers left us late the next day. We'd climbed a steep pass above Akrotiri and watched as the legionnaires descended to the lake below. We were far beyond Antioch and even farther from Iconium.

We plodded along the road for days. I thought often of Cassandra. I loved her more with every lonely step and longed to see her again, but my hope wavered. In resignation, I prayed, "Fulfill your will in Cassandra's life and in mine, Lord. If that means separate lives in your service, so be it."

We trekked on rocky roads through sparsely treed hills until I saw what I thought was a giant monument towering above the settlement of Ipsus. It turned out to be a mountain with sides too steep for even a wild goat to climb. A formidable stone fortress capped the crag. As we neared the city gates, we passed a wide trail cut into the mountainside with steps rising to the edifice.

"That fortress has been used for a thousand years," Silas said. "Now the Roman army uses it to guard the approaches to the city. The fields nearby are the site of the great battle between Alexander's successors. Antigonus lost his ambitions and his life there."

I stood in the middle of the road and stared at the lofty stronghold, mesmerized by its enormous height. It was so steep I could see only the outer walls and a legion's red pennant. A trumpet sounded and the thunderous tramp of many feet behind broke my concentration.

Silas shouted, "Timothy!" A legionnaire's shield struck me on the shoulder and threw me to the ground. Booted feet pounded by, rank after rank. Silas and Paul tugged me off the road.

I gripped my shoulder and groaned. "What's happening?" I asked.

"Roman guards from the fort," Paul said. "Something's stirred them up. They don't force-march unless there's serious trouble."

"But they're going north, on the road we'll be on. Are we in danger? I mean, other than from the Romans," I joked. "My shoulder's all right, by the way, thanks for asking."

Silas helped me to my feet. "Sorry, Timothy."

"We're all in danger," came a voice. Across the road, a young man in a pleb's blue tunic stood at the bottom of the mountain steps. "I've just come form the fort," he said. The man patted his sack. "Daily bread delivery. I heard their commander."

Silas pulled a coin from his purse. "Tell us," he said. "Where's the trouble? How far north?"

"Don't know, but it's the Gauls, as usual." He handed Silas a loaf as he took the coin. "They raid all over the frontiers of Bithynia. Thank the gods, they don't come this far south, or so close to an armed fortress."

"That's our route," I said. "Straight into danger. God, keep us safe."

"Follow the soldiers' route," the man said. "Stay on this road and stay overnight in cities or Roman outposts. Don't be alone."

"Wise words," Paul said. "We do ourselves no good dwelling on danger. We'll stay on this road when we leave Ipsus. But first we need lodging."

Silas asked where a tent-maker lived, where we could offer our services in exchange for shelter. We found ourselves with Lucius and Helen, strangers to us but hospitable. They lived and worked in a shop on a corner of a three story building. Silas and I mended tents while Paul wove cloth in the candlelit room. While Helen spun wool, she hummed tunes like the ones Mother had sung to me as a child.

Lucius sat on a sturdy three-legged stool. His beard rested halfway down his chest and his arms just reached around his belly as he forced his awl through tent cloth. His voice rumbled like hoofbeats. "You know of the tortoise's race with a hare?" His narrow eyes looked past his work and glanced at us.

I laughed. "Why would a tortoise race a hare?"

While he sewed, Lucius told us the tale of the patient tortoise and the confident hare. Both sewing and story-telling were second nature to him, but he stopped work at the story's climax. He looked at us over his sewing and said, "When the hare awoke from his nap, he saw the tortoise just near the winning-post and couldn't finish in time to win the race." Then he roared with laughter and we all joined him.

"The story's from near here," he said. "Aesop from Cotyaeum told it first and put these words in the tortoise' mouth at the end: 'Slow but steady wins the race.'"

He told us story after story and we laughed until our sides hurt. He ended with the tale of the wolf in sheep's clothing.

"Jesus told a story like that," Silas said. "To warn against false teachers."

"But He held to the truth, like no other," Paul said.

"Truth is this," Lucius said. "A man must make his way in the world by whatever means and the gods have no say in right or wrong. They do what they will. So do I. Drive a hard bargain, I do, and if I cheat," he said, laughing, "it's good for business. Everyone does it."

"You sound like a wolf in sheep's clothing, Lucius," I said. "Jesus' way is better. It's makes enemies into friends."

He pushed himself up from his stool and stretched his back. "My belly grumbles its need. We're not high-born, so come, sit with us while we eat."

He took a clumsy step toward the table and I saw that his left leg was made of wood below the knee.

"What happened to your leg?" I asked.

"Ah," he said. "Don't be shocked my friend. It's no worse than others have suffered hereabouts. Gauls attack without warning. They steal our cattle, our tools, even our food and women."

Lucius steadied himself and eased his body into the chair. His leg stuck straight out under the table. He scowled ferociously at me. "Now, you be careful where you sit," he said. "If you jam my leg I'll sit on you and crush you like an eggshell."

"I'm sorry," I said. "I'll take care."

My face must have turned white because he laughed and pointed.

"You look like a ghost, my friend. Rest easy. I mean nothing by it. Just warnin' you. Now sit. Eat."

Silas spread our bread, figs and olives out on the table and Helen added cheese, sardines and watered wine. While we ate, Lucius told us of the Gauls' vicious assaults.

"They hide in the hills, out of range of Roman legions. You won't see them till they're on you."

Paul raised his brow at Silas and me and dipped some bread in the sardines' oil.

"Nearly lost Helen years past," Lucius went on. "A giant of a Gaul had her pinned with his hands on her throat. I kicked him off. He swung his sword and hacked off my leg. I fell atop him and strangled him to death while the blood poured from my leg. I passed out."

"Enough dwelling on the past," Helen said. "We make do now."

She put dessert on the table. "This is our specialty: Cream, churned thick as butter and topped with fruit and nuts. I only use milk from cows that have grazed on poppies."

The sweet cream slipped down my throat like nectar and took away my shoulder's pain. It was a delight like none I'd experienced before. I slept well that night curled up in my bedding on the floor.

Silas gave Lucius a few coins when we left the next morning.

"You're a good host, Lucius," Silas said, "and Helen's cream dessert was worth more than our tent-making labour. May the coins make you think well of us. Next time you hear of Jesus, listen closely, my friend."

Lucius propped his huge body in his doorway. "I make no promise," he said, "but peace be with you, and safety." He pointed into the distance. "You'll know your destination when you see the mountain."

"God's peace," I said, "and safety. Fare well."

A short distance beyond Ipsos we met the junction with the road west to Smyrna, but we continued north toward Aezani. Late spring weather in the high country was unpredictable. Wind and rain assaulted us most of the morning. When it subsided before midday, the air stayed cold and the sky dark. My soaked clothes hung like heavy sacks of grain. My sandals chafed my ankles. My feet ached with every step.

Rock faces beside the steep road were blanketed in wet moss and lichen. Silas huddled into his wool coat. "I've never been so cold this late in spring."

"This chill may have a more ominous source," Paul said. "Look there, tombs in the rock."

"And a cave behind them," Silas said. "Shelter!"

The tombs were framed with carvings, doorways to the realm of the dead. I ran my finger over an inscription that named the one buried inside. Faded scratches in the stones listed personal possessions, a mirror and baskets of wool, as if the woman buried there still existed between death and life. Cold air whispered about my neck and ears like voices of the dead.

"Here, look," Paul called. "Eagles, lions and bulls mark the men's tombs."

Silas found a sarcophagus carved with pictures of the Greeks and Amazons at war. "There may be more of these in the cave where it'll be dry. Let's look."

I only wanted a fire to dry my clothes and warm my cold body. Why would Silas want to enter a dark, damp cave full of tombs? Who knew what demons might be there?

Just then a shriek echoed from the hills beyond the tombs. Blue-faced men in animal skins screamed and waved their swords and knives as they ran straight at us across the broad hillside.

"Gauls!" Silas shouted. "Into the cave, quick! They won't follow us into the realm of the dead."

I hustled through the low entrance. Drops of icy water fell on my neck, cobwebs brushed my face. The dank, musty air of the darkness choked. My legs shook from cold and terror.

"Pray, my friends." Paul's voice echoed off the walls. I jumped, banging my head on the rocks above. "We tempt dark forces in here," Paul continued. "The presence of Christ protects us. Pray!"

Paul's warning stopped me at the edge of a deep hole that would have swallowed us up. The screams from outside came closer. We peered into the depths. On ledges around the hole's perimeter and on shelves below, stood figurines of the area's goddess, Kybele. At the pit's bottom, bones lay scattered about. The Gauls shouted and argued outside and Ruth brayed in panic.

"They're afraid," Silas said. "They believe spirits haunt the tombs."

At the cave mouth, the blue-faced brigands shook their weapons at each other and at us.

"I have no fear of the dead," Silas said, "or the impotent gods that attend them." Then he shouted at the Gauls, "Why do you look for the living among the dead?" His words bounced off the cavern walls.

"Timothy," he said. "That's what the angels said to the women who went to our master's tomb."

He shouted at the Gauls again, "He is not here! He is risen!"

The cave held the idols and symbols of false religion and helpless gods, I thought as I pondered Silas' words. Their strength had been crushed by the resurrection.

The voices outside stopped. The exit was clear.

My body shook from the icy chill, even though I wrapped my arms around myself and rubbed my chest with a fury. "I'm so cold," I said. "We need a fire."

"We can't stay here," Paul said, "and I don't hear the Gauls outside. Can we go?"

Silas stepped into the daylight. He peered beyond the entrance then turned back to us. "No Gauls. Wait, I'll look further."

He disappeared from view. I sneezed from the cold wind rushing into the cave.

"I have to get out of here," I said. I burst past Paul and stumbled out of the cave and past the sarcophagus. Paul followed right behind me.

I heard a distant trumpet and the steady tramp of army boots. Silas pointed along the road. A troop of Roman legionnaires marched toward us. Their commander shouted something and the soldiers doubled their pace. At a second command they turned off the road, straight toward the mountains where I saw the back ends of the Gauls running up the hills.

We were alone. Rain had stopped falling from the brightening sky. Paul threw a blanket from the cart over my shoulders. "Are you warm enough to continue, my son?" he asked.

"If we set a fast pace I'll warm up." I climbed back to the road and our mule-cart and took Ruth's reins.

Silas dug into the provisions and fed her a handful of grain.

We trekked toward Aezani's gates as fast as Ruth would pull. We stopped only to get more supplies from the market. North of Aezani, we settled into a steady pace and let the afternoon sun warm us and dry our clothes.

At a lake near Cotyaeum, there was a garrisoned Roman postal station where we camped with a caravan of merchants. We stayed the next day to rest from our dangerous and relentless journey. Swans flapped their wings along the surface of the water, then soared into the air and flew north. We caught fish and ate ripe almonds from trees on the shore. A single day of calm didn't do much for our tired bodies, but it refreshed our souls.

We left with renewed energy and turned west from Cotyaeum to stay with the caravan.

Four days later, not long after leaving another Roman garrison, I saw the mountain. We'd struggled to the top of a high pass above the trees. The slope fell away to the north. A light rainfall moistened the plants and below us, countless treed hills flowed like waves of the sea to where Olympus' snowcapped peak brushed the pale blue heavens. From here all the streams led north, to Mysia and Bithynia. I turned Ruth off the road and pointed into the distance. "Paul, Silas, look ... the wilderness we've searched for."

"Finally I see it with my own eyes," Paul said. "There we'll till the soil, sow the seed, and reap the harvest of men and women for Jesus." He dropped to his knees and prayed.

"I've never seen such majesty," Silas said. "Surely, with this beauty to remind people of the creator, many will choose to believe his son."

Paul gazed at the mountains of Bithynia while the last wagons of the caravan passed by. We stood alone with miles of mountainous, rocky roads ahead and a foreign people we wouldn't understand. Ruth brayed, tugged the cart to a clump of long moist grass and grazed.

"Paul," I asked. "Will they understand us? Are we safe from Gauls? How can we serve the master in that land?"

"In the market," Paul said. "Just as we did in Lystra. Merchants and traders will understand Greek."

He placed a hand on Silas' shoulder and the other on mine. "There's no need for fear, my friends. The Lord himself guided me here. He'll keep us in the shadow of his wings."

18

Danger from Floods

WE STRUGGLED DOWN THE NARROW, ROCKY ROAD TOWARD BYTHINIA. Ruth dug in her hooves and we braced ourselves against the cart to keep it from running away. We soon met a company of travellers struggling up the hill toward us, with a covered carriage drawn by donkeys. Two swarthy men with long hair and full beards held the reins. One carried a curved sword slung over his shoulder. Their baggy Thracian pants and white shirts were dirty and torn. They wore sleeveless tunics and long sashes around their waists. A young woman walked by the cart. A vest with gold needlework covered her tattered white cotton underdress and she'd tied a stained patterned scarf around her head. From inside the carriage, I heard a woman sobbing and a man groaning.

We moved to the side of the road to let them pass and the carriage stopped in its progress up the hill. Inside lay an old man on a pallet with a woman by his side.

Paul called to them in common Greek, "Do you need help?"

The man with the sword gripped its handle. "Trouble. Bad trouble," he said. "Raided. Burned. Three days past. Father hurt bad. We need safety. To rest. To heal."

"We have no weapons," Paul said. "We'll take you to safety. A postal station and inn. Licensed and garrisoned. Back up so we can turn our cart and lead."

As they manoeuvred their wagon, I saw that the other man had only one useful arm, the left one was withered and limp. But he was strong and with our help we managed the wagons. Paul and I stayed with the men and pushed the caravan from behind. Silas led Ruth up the steep road.

The two young men were Zipoates and Ziaelas. Their mother, Prusia, lifted the caravan's curtain and spoke in a language we didn't understand, though we could tell she was thanking us. The young woman who now drove the wagon was Maria, named after her father, Marius. Zipoates thanked us, speaking in passable Greek.

"Two nights past. Blazing light fill our house," he said. "I see through the trees, my uncle's home. In flames. We flee from blaze. Only us, our caravan, our donkeys. I hear screams. Cries. We no look back. Find cave. Hide all day. All night."

Zipoates pressed his hands to his ears and shook his head. "Father, brother, me. We go back." He stared at me out of tearful black eyes.

"Nothing. Ashes, black, charred timbers. Father search ruins. Fall. Scream. Chest bad. No breathe."

I thought of my father, when he swung his sledge hammer and fell down dead. Tears came to my eyes. Their father lay dying inside the caravan. Could God save him?

"Paul," I said, "Help Marius. Go inside. Maybe it's not too late."

I boosted Paul into the caravan and watched through the open curtain as he examined Marius. He lightly touched a massive dark bruise that covered his side and chest. Marius groaned.

"Timothy, bring myrrh from my bag and mix it with oil. The paste will help these wounds heal."

When I mixed the ointment, it smelled like wet earth and damp wood. Paul gave the paste to Prusia. "Take the paste and spread it on his bruises." He took a little from the jar and showed her what to do.

Prusia's gentle touch quieted the groaning and soon the poor man was asleep.

"The injuries we see will mend," Paul whispered to me. "We have nothing for the injuries within. Pray for God to heal Marius."

We prayed as we pushed the wagon to the main road. At the junction, we stopped to rest and water the animals.

Silas brought water and bread. Ziaelos, with his head in his hand, sat beside Paul "I've seen men die from injuries like these," Paul said. "We've prayed. Now it's in God's hands."

Ziaelos put his hand on Paul's shoulder and boosted himself to his feet. "If your God saves Father, he'll be my God, too."

We carried on to the garrison and camped there setting our cart near Marius' wagon and Silas built a fire in the space between the two. We made a meal of lentils, cheese and bread. Maria brought cabbage and artichoke and Zipoates roasted a hare he'd snared overnight. Prusia stayed in the carriage with Marius. Maria took food to her but returned with it untouched. She sat with us and wiped her tears while we ate in silence.

The setting sun cast a red glow over the campsite as we cleaned up the last of our meal. Maria shuffled to the carriage and drew the canvas apart. She stopped on the bottom step of the little ladder and gasped. Ziaelas rushed over and held her. "Be brave, sister," he said. "We must be brave."

Prusia said something in a strong voice and Maria sobbed and covered her face. Ziaelas climbed the steps and looked inside. I heard Marius' deep voice from within the carriage and Prusia talking with him.

Ziaelas caught his breath. "It's Father! He's awake. He is strong. He is well. Come. We beg you. You healed Father. You are mighty."

Zipoates had been stoking the fire. He stood up when he heard Ziaelas.

"Zipoates," Paul said, "tell your family this is done by God alone. We're his servants. These wonders can happen in your life, but you must choose the way of Jesus."

"Anything," he said. "We have nothing more to lose. There is life to gain. Your God is like no other."

He went into the wagon and I heard excited voices.

Marius stepped through the canvas entry. He climbed down the ladder with his sons' help. At the bottom, he lifted his arms. "Come, I am well!" he shouted. "We must celebrate. We must dance!"

Ziaelos reached into the carriage for a *daouli*, a two-headed drum then placed it between his knees and began a quick, steady beat with a stick in his good right hand, deftly swinging it between the two drumheads to accent the beat.

Maria played a *gaida*, made out of a bladder of skins that blew air into reed-pipes as it was squeezed between her arm and body. It made a high drone along with its melody. Zipoates played a reeded instrument called a *klarino*.

Prusia and Marius pulled us into a circle and we danced. We held each other by a belt or sash, or just a piece of clothing and danced rhythmically in a circle. It wasn't very different from some of the dances I'd enjoyed in Lystra at weddings. We finished with a whoop of joy and laughter, and collapsed around the fire.

Paul told the story of Jesus at the wedding feast. "Jesus was good news," he said.

"Good news," Marius said. "You bring good news. You bring healing. You bring love for strangers. Your God is good."

"He's your God too, Marius," Paul said. "Learn from Him. Go with us into Bithynia. Together we'll bring his story to your people."

"First you must teach us," Marius said.

"Many years ago," Paul began, "a young woman, Mary, in the town of Nazareth was betrothed to the village carpenter, a man named Joseph..."

I listened as I watched heaven's glorious array above us. I stared at the constellations, Castor and Pollux, the twins, low in the west, soon to disappear behind the hills. High in the sky shone Cassiopeia and a bright wanderer, probably Jupiter. Soon I wrapped my bedroll about me and fell asleep by the fire, wondering at the immensity of God's amazing creation.

I was first up in the morning. The fields were heavy with dew under a cloudy sky. Paul secured our load while I hitched Ruth to the cart, then I helped yoke Marius' donkeys to their wagon. While I was finishing, travellers arrived at the inn.

There were three of them and a heavily-burdened donkey. The man in front wore a cloth around his head in the old Hebrew style and his tunic had the characteristic Judean fringes.

"*Shalom, boker tov,*" I said. "I'm Timothy."

He stood by his beast and extended his hand. "Ah, fellow Jews. May Jehovah be with you in your travels." He was clean-shaven and his eyes lacked emotion.

"I'm Procorus," he said, "and these are my companions, Philios and Marcion."

I greeted each of them. "You're early to the inn," I said. "Surely you didn't travel through the night?"

"We were too slow to reach here before dark," Procorus said. "Camped by the road and started at first light. Haven't eaten or drunk, but thank Jehovah, he kept us safe. We'll press on to Nicomedia, Bithynia's chief city, once we've eaten."

The other two men began searching through their packs. They retrieved flagons of drink, and cheese and bread.

Paul offered them some dried lamb. "We've been on that road," he said. "It's dangerous." He pointed to Marius and his family. These Thracians were burned out of their home by marauding Gauls. You must be on your guard, or choose another road."

The stranger cut a hunk of cured lamb and passed it to one of the others. "There is only one way for us. We must reach Nicomedia."

"Then we'll travel with you," Paul offered. "It'll be safer for all."

Silas and Zipoates had been loading the wagon. They joined us as we talked with the travellers.

The instant Silas saw their leader, he exclaimed, "Procorus! How is this?" He gripped Procorus in a huge embrace, then held him at arm's length. "You ... here? I last saw you in Jerusalem twelve, thirteen years ago. Then you left and went to Alexandria, wasn't it?"

"What a memory, Silas! I knew you were in Galatia, but not that you were going north. So this must be Timothy who I've heard so much about, and our brother in the gospel, Paul. I've been longing to meet you both, but I have a special reason to speak with you, Paul. I have to tell you what the master's done in my heart."

"Well, I'm all ears," Paul said. "Unless I'm mistaken, Procorus, we've never met so it's a mystery why you'd have words for me. Let's talk as we travel."

Marius and all his family wanted to hear the story, but one of them needed to tend the donkeys. Zipoates had already hitched them to the wagon and waited to set off.

"Zipoates," Marius said, "Look to the wagon."

Zipoates goaded his donkeys and the wagon lurched forward. Our cart was next and Procorus' party followed with their donkey. Silas led Ruth while I listened to Procorus. "I was one of the seven chosen to oversee the food distribution to believing widows in Jerusalem," he began. "We were appointed by Jesus' twelve closest followers. They searched out Spirit-filled, wise men, and to my surprise I was included with Stephen and the others."

Procorus paused to look at each of us when he said this: "You see, I didn't consider myself of the same class as the others, so I took my responsibilities more seriously and tried very hard to impress them. I've since learned that only Jesus' opinion matters. Our numbers grew so quickly in Jerusalem that the Synagogue of the Freedmen stirred up the people and the Sanhedrin against my uncle, Stephen. They stoned him to death."

He pointed at Paul, who walked with his head down. "You were there. Standing with the men of the Tarsus synagogue. You railed against my uncle."

Paul looked up. His face was pale, his mouth curled into a frown. Tears formed in his eyes. He looked frightened, like a mongrel waiting to be beaten.

Procorus put his arm around Paul's shoulder. He raised his voice like a preacher. "I was in Alexandria when the news came that you, who once persecuted us, had become a follower of Jesus! I rejoiced and praised God for his surprising grace. Now, we are brothers, teaching the gospel in this neglected land. Long ago I forgave you, Paul, but I've never had the chance to tell you face to face."

Paul embraced Procorus. "I'm the worst of sinners," Paul said. "Your forgiveness means everything to me."

Procorus released Paul. "Your name has become a rallying call for us all. Many of the Jerusalem Christians left during your persecution and more have left recently. Bartholomew to Lycaonia, Thomas to Ethiopia, Andrew to Scythia north of the Pontus Euxinus and Philip to Phrygia. James, the master's brother, is still in Jerusalem. Luke has sailed from Antioch along the Aegean coast to Troas. They're spreading the good news all over the world.

"Your example is an inspiration. You, who once persecuted us, preach with the courage to be beaten for the gospel. Surely, I can do the same.

"They told me you'd be in Galatia," he continued, "or maybe Asia or Greece. But here you are, on the road with me. Let's make a powerful team for the master."

"Two enemies, now one in Jesus' work!" shouted Marius. "Many will come to hear your stories. I must tell Zipoates." He rushed back to the wagon and began an animated discussion with his son.

A breeze stirred the grasses by the road and a few shafts of light broke through the clouds. Paul stood a little taller now and walked more quickly. His face was sombre, but the tears were gone.

"Procorus, I can't thank you enough for your forgiveness. I'm worthy of neither your kindness nor your partnership. We could, by God's grace, serve him well together, but the Spirit is now whispering to me that our small company won't enter Bithynia. God has brought us together and I'm tempted by your plan, but I know by his inner voice we have to move on."

Paul looked toward Olympus' sunlit, snow-covered peak. "It's

God's plan for you, not me, to bring the gospel to this region. He'll do great things through you. I'll pray and trust that the master will bring us together again."

"We would have made such a team!" Procorus said. "But if the Spirit leads you elsewhere, I can't oppose him. Thank God I've met you. We're at peace with one another. Jehovah will bless you, my brother."

Marius had returned. When he heard that we were not going to Bithynia, he went back to his wagon. He shook his head when he talked with Zipoates then went into the carriage.

We carried on a little further to the crossroads where Procorus would continue to Bithynia and we'd turn west toward Mysia. To the north the sky had cleared around Olympus and its white-crowned peak filled the horizon. The road ahead, clear of other travellers, pointed straight to the mountain.

Paul stood by Procorus. "There's your path. Remember, 'how beautiful on the mountains are the feet of those who bring good news.' I know God will be with you. I feel it in my heart."

Silas and I were telling Procorus' companions that we'd been warned about raiding Gauls in the region they'd be travelling, when Marius and his sons marched past.

Marius called out, "Paul, we've decided to go with Procorus. We can be Jesus' voice to our people."

Zipoates and Ziaelas stood at his side. "We're agreed on this," said Ziaelos. He pointed back to the wagon where the women waited.

"It's God's will," he said.

Paul raised his arms. "Bless God the Father and his Son, that they'd bring you together with Procorus to take his message to your own people. Now his plan is clear. Go with God, my brothers. Serve him with all your minds, hearts and strength."

So we parted at the Bithynian road and turned west toward Mysia and the Aegean Sea, just the three of us once again.

19

Trimalchio

I DIDN'T UNDERSTAND PAUL'S SUDDEN CHANGE OF PLAN. ONLY A FEW days before, he'd been convinced that God was leading us to bring the good news to Bithynia.

I walked beside him. "What changed your mind, Paul? I thought the Spirit was guiding."

"Perhaps not as we thought, Timothy. The master brought us here to help Marius' family. The Spirit took away my passion for Bithynia the moment Procorus told me his plans to minister there. I don't always understand the Spirit's leading my friend, but I hope I'll always recognize it and obey. Do you agree?"

"Yes, of course. I just needed you to explain. You've helped me trust the master's voice in me. I trust it in you too."

We slogged through two days of steady rain. On the third day the sky cleared and Olympus towered over the northern hills once again. I felt an urge to run ahead and test my endurance. I stripped to a tunic and waist-cloth, took a bag of nuts and fruit and started off, a relaxed run to warm up and then faster. I splashed along the wet trails and leaped the big puddles. I lost track of the *stade* markers and ran until the sun was overhead, then took a break at a stream that gushed down the mountainside, north toward the Propontus.

The stream had breached its banks and flowed right over the wooden bridge that across it.

Powerful waves drove against the bridge. It could be destroyed before Paul and Silas arrived. I settled down to rest a short distance away where I could keep an eye on it.

I drank from a nearby brook and lunched on the fruit and nuts. Once rested, I ran back to Paul and Silas. We made it to the flooding stream before nightfall.

The bridge was gone. Timbers sat like a clumsy stack of firewood at the bottom of the hill and the stream roared down the canyon.

"Timothy, you chose wisely," Paul shouted over the noise. "You could have been swept away if you'd tried to cross."

"Thank God you came back. Every day you become more indispensable to me."

For our camp, Paul chose a place well away from the stream, below a rock outcrop that would protect us from tumbling rocks or debris.

Overnight, clouds came and rains began again. They beat against the tent all night. By morning it was clear that there was no chance of crossing the stream by the path we were on. I hiked down the hill to see if there was a quieter spot where we could cross. Far below, the slope flattened and the stream shallowed, flooding the small plain. If we got the cart and mule down the hillside, we could cross and make our way back up to the path.

We unpacked the cart, leaving the heaviest items behind the outcrop, then hitched Ruth facing the cart. Silas and I supported the back of the cart while Paul tended Ruth. We eased the cart over the hill, back first. I dug my heels into the rocky hillside and fumbled for a strong grip. Several times the ground gave way. Each time, I was sure the cart would tumble over me and crush me beneath it. But Paul heaved back on Ruth's reins and she stopped the cart.

At the bottom, I fell beside to the ground, soaked and muddy. I let the rain wash me clean.

Paul released Ruth from her traces. She lapped water from the puddles, then grazed on the wet grass.

Holding on to the cart, Paul eased himself around to the back where he climbed into the box and lay there.

Silas slogged through the water and stood beside Paul. "Are you all right?" he asked.

"No." Paul said. "My back screams with pain. Let me rest."

"Rest then. The rain's stopping. Timothy and I can retrieve our supplies."

We climbed back to the rocky outcrop, brought everything to the bottom of the slope and packed it in the wagon with Paul. We hitched Ruth to the cart. As we prepared to cross the stream we heard a frantic shout. Rocks thudded down the hillside behind us.

Someone was tumbling head over heels down the hill. He slid on his backside on the wet mud and finally jammed his feet into the slope. He pitched forward with a loud "Whoooop!" and fell face first into the water, right in front of the cart. He startled Ruth who reared and jerked the wagon forward over him. When the man lifted his head he looked through a forest of mule legs and wagon wheels, spit out a plume of water and broke into gales of laughter.

"My Lord Zeus, what a thrill!" he cried. "My bones are in one piece and my thick skull intact, but oh, my back hurts. Help me, fellow travellers. I'll need some bandaging."

Silas was already at his side and helped him out of the stream. Muddy water poured off his red hair and beard. We stood him up. His tunic was torn and he had bruises and scrapes on his back from top to bottom.

"Who are you?" I asked, as we cleaned the mud from the sores and bandaged them.

He looked at me with clear blue eyes. In spite of his wounds, his mouth twisted halfway between mockery and glee. "By the gods, that's one slippery slope. I don't know what I'd have done if you'd not been here. I carry an important contract for my master. I'm to make Troas in five days or my name's mud. Not far from the truth, to look at me. Too fast comin' down and lost my footing. Thank Apollo I ain't dead." He looked up at the road and down at the pool of water around us. My name's Trimalchio. Now, can I take you through the waters? 'Tis the least I can do."

"We need help, Trimalchio," I said. "I'm Timothy. This is Paul. He's hurt his back. Silas and I could never get this cart back to the road without you. You're a gift from God."

"And you," Trimalchio said, gripping my arm. "The gods have smiled on us in this calamity. Let's get to work."

The current was strong and might easily have washed us away without Trimalchio's help. We reached the other side and worked our way up the slope to our original path, then rested. We ate a small meal below a rocky overhang.

Silas helped Paul out of the cart and made him comfortable. Trimalchio built a fire and draped his torn tunic over a branch near the flames.

"I'll mend that when it's dry, Trimalchio," Paul said. "I can still be of some use in spite of my back."

"Very well, my friend. We serve one another. I'm slave to Andronicus, merchant of Cotyaeum. He bought me when I was a child. I must reach Troas to get the signature of ship captain, Aquius Trio, to ensure safe and timely passage."

"You could have been killed in that fall," Silas said. "Shouldn't you be more careful with that contract?"

"True," Trimalchio said. "There's dangers on the road and I've had my life threatened many times. Storms, rockfalls, bandits, even fellow travellers'd rob you blind. But I've survived. The gods favor me, I say. I put my life in their hands, but hold a knife in mine at night against the dangers."

"And do the gods always help you?" I asked. "They didn't prevent your fall."

He roared with laughter. "No, they didn't, curse 'em! You're right. I don't know why I trust the gods. But if they be not true, I've nothing."

"Our God is true, Trimalchio," Paul said. "He's proven himself many times. He's brought you here so we can tell you his story. I know you need to get to Troas, but journey with us a little, so we can tell you about Jesus. He lives within us. He'll live in you if you choose him."

"Choose, now that's a strange word. I'm a slave. I don't get to choose. I have to invoke my master's gods. One god's as good as another, or as useless."

"Your gods are made of stone." Paul countered. "They can't leave their altars to answer your prayers. Our God is flesh and Spirit. Your gods want sacrifice. You must beg their favor. Our God is our sacrifice and asks only for our trust."

Trimalchio stood and shook his head. "You've told me nothing to convince me, Paul. If your god's real, let him show himself. When that happens, I'll trust him. I must be off. Farewell my friends, and thanks for your help. I'll look for you in Troas or on the road when I return."

Paul held up his hand. "Wait, Trimalchio. Timothy will run with you. You'll be good companions, I'm sure, and he can return to us in the morning. You won't get much further. The sun's setting soon."

I packed some food and a cover for the night and off we went. It looked as though clear skies might last until morning. Trimalchio said we weren't on the main Roman road from Syria to the Aegean, which lay further south, but on a secondary road from Cotyaeum to the coast at Adramyttium. The section we ran was a rocky path, muddy and slippery from the rain.

Trimalchio set a reasonable pace, quick, but cautious of the mud. His presence made the time go quickly and it seemed only minutes before the gathering shadows forced us to find a place to camp and settle for the night.

Trimalchio took a knife and twine from his bag. He went a short distance to an animal trail and set a snare. In the centre of it, he put some grain from his pack. "If the gods be with us and the sun do rise, we'll have fresh meat at dawn."

We made ourselves comfortable in our bedding and Trimalchio told me about his life as a slave.

"In Cotyaeum, work was mostly loading and unloading goods that came by caravan and left on Andronicus' wagons," he told me. "I love the journeys. My master trusts me to courier his most important documents. On the road I feel free. I run all day, find a hidden site at night and sleep under the stars. Even in the worst weather there's beauty in the hills and vales, streams and lakes. I almost never camp with others on the way. I've been robbed, beaten, and cheated of my possessions. When I'm alone, I'm safe. I call on Hermes. Sometimes he helps me."

"My friend Kopries was born with weak legs," I said, "but my God gave him strong legs and now he walks. Paul was struck blind and Jesus healed him."

"Is this true? Do you sell medicine at great cost and flee before you're caught? I know travellers like you."

He looked angry. "I thought I could trust you," he said.

"You can, Trimalchio. I don't want your money. I won't take anything from you. I want to give you something."

"What would you give?"

I would give you the love of Jesus, my God, my healer, my protector."

"He must prove himself before I trust."

"He will," I said.

We ran together until noon the next day, parting after sharing the last of the partridge he caught in the snare. He carried on toward the coast and I retraced my steps to Paul and Silas, meeting them just before nightfall. The three of us prayed for Trimalchio. I wanted to see him again, but realized there was little chance of that.

Late the next day, Paul climbed into the cart, unable to keep the pace we'd set.

"Are you in pain?" I asked.

"My hips and back hurt with every step. Working the cart down the hill put more strain on these old bones than they can handle. I'm past the days I could run like you, and today I can't even keep up with poor Ruth. If there's no improvement, we'll have to change our plans."

"Is there anything I can do?" I asked.

"There's not much anyone can do but make me comfortable. Now help me find a suitable place on this hard ground."

I lay my sheepskin overcoat on the ground for Paul. Silas and I packed other garments under him where he felt the most pain.

In the morning Paul could barely move. He couldn't put any weight on his hips and his back was in excruciating pain. We moved him to the cart and made him comfortable, but he cried out at every bump that jostled the cart. I offered to run ahead and see if I could find a town where we could get medical help.

"Timothy," Paul said, "I trust you. Silas and I will keep to the main road and stay in sight when we camp so you can find us when you return. Leave a message at each inn or village you pass until you reach Adramyttium. There's money in this bag. Use it wisely and don't display it needlessly. Trust no one. The master will be with you to strengthen and protect you. We'll see you in a few days, my son."

Paul's words lifted a great weight from me. He trusted me and had forgiven my mistakes. I'd find a doctor and bring him to Paul.

I set a brisk pace to reach the coast within two days. Like Trimalchio, I kept to myself on the road and at night so I met with no trouble all the way to Adramyttium and arrived early on the third day. I found the market and bought salted fish. As I was paying the fishmonger, I heard a call: "Whooop Timothy!"

I knew it was Trimalchio. I'd kept my eye out for him hoping we'd meet again. I turned toward his voice and noticed that the whole market had stopped at his strange greeting.

"You've made good time, my friend," he cried out. "Where are your companions?"

"On the road. Paul hurt his back coming through the flood. I've come ahead to find a doctor."

"Then my duty is to help, as you helped me at the river. I met a *medicus* in Troas when I gave my master's contract to Aquius Trio. I'd taken off my bandages and tunic for the sun to dry my wounds. The doctor was leaving another ship and saw my bruises and scrapes. He set to rubbing some balm into the sores. I told him I couldn't pay as I am a slave and he spoke the strangest words to me. 'I too am a slave.' I have to tell you, Tim, he looked no slave to me. He's well dressed and bobbed to by Aquius Trio and his sailors. They give no quarter to slaves. But he set me right. 'I am a slave of Jesus, my master,' he said. 'If you'll allow me, I'll heal your wounds for no cost. Slave for slave, we must stick together.' You told me about this Jesus, Tim, and here's this stranger, a doctor no less, spoke of the same man and treated my wounds. He calls himself Luke. When I told him where I'd been, he asked if I'd seen three men travelling together. Then, amazing it were, he describes you and Paul and Silas. He's staying in Assos not a half-day's run from here?"

"Trimalchio, we must go to Luke now! Don't you see? God brought this to pass. He's answered my prayers. Not only is there a physician near, but he knows Paul. This is Jesus' work."

"Tim, this is perilous strange. I must think on it. We'll eat, then to Assos and no delay. Tell me more later."

We reached Assos at midday. Trimalchio took me to the roadside inn where he'd last seen Luke. We found him at a taberna nearby. He was an imposing man, tall and straight-backed. His hair was graying, but thick, swept back to reveal a fresh, open face and honest smile.

Trimalchio bowed. "Doctor, I bring Timothy. He needs your help."

"He looked me over calmly, stroking his trim beard. "Would you be Timothy of Lystra who's been with Paul and Silas?"

I blinked and nodded.

"Don't be surprised," he said. "I've known of you since Paul and Silas left Antioch in the spring. Paul told me about the remarkable young man from Lystra that he wanted to recruit. I see he's succeeded." He shook my hand in a strong grip.

"Where are they?" he asked. "The church asked me to watch for them."

"They're near, just days along the Cotyaeum road. Paul's in great pain. Can you help?"

"We'll see," he said. "Let me gather my medicines and instruments. You buy food and drink for our journey and for Paul and Silas."

Trimalchio traveled with us as far as Adramyttium to wait for his master's shipment. Luke and I retraced my steps hoping to meet up with Paul and Silas before nightfall the next day.

"How do you know Paul?" I asked as we marched stride for stride along the road.

"I first met him in Tarsus where I studied medicine. We met again in Syrian Antioch, where there's a large assembly of Christians. When he and Silas left to trek overland to Derbe, I hired on as a ship's physician and sailed, by stages to Troas."

"All in God's plan," I said.

"He never ceases to amaze."

When we reached Paul and Silas, they were in a grassy field. Paul was lying in the cart, his skin pale and sweaty. Our greetings were brief. Luke took charge immediately.

"Silas, help me with Paul," he ordered. "Timothy, set up camp in a sheltered spot and prepare a soft bed."

We lay Paul on straw bedding and Luke went to work. He bent Paul's legs into various positions, asking him where he felt pain. Occasionally he'd press on a muscle or rub a bone to see if it hurt.

He pointed to a swollen area low on Paul's back. "See here, Timothy," he said. He touched the swelling and Paul shrunk away with a moan.

Luke kept his hand on the bruised area. "Bones of the spine are sometimes forced out of place by stress or injury according to Cornelius Celsus of Rome. That's what we have here. It may be possible to put them back in position."

I helped him move Paul onto his side. Luke thrust his hand against the swelling. Paul let out a small groan and a prolonged sigh, "Aaaah."

"Yes," Luke said. "Something beneficial happened there, I think. Now, carefully, Timothy, Silas, roll Paul onto his back." Luke supported Paul's back while we rolled him over.

"Timothy, " he said, "build a fire and find some flat, smooth stones. Warm them in the fire, then bring them to me."

Luke made Paul as comfortable as he could. "Don't move. Stay on your back," he said.

I helped Paul eat some fish and bread until Luke decided the stones were warm enough, He slipped them carefully under Paul in the small of his back alongside the spine. "Normally, I'd prescribe a visit to the baths or a spa," he said, "but that's impossible. The stones' heat will help your back muscles rest and recover."

Paul did seem to sleep well that night. In the morning he raised himself gingerly with Luke's help and took a few steps. "It does feel better," he said. "Will I be able to carry on as normal?"

"Perhaps, but the moment the pain sharpens, you must stop and rest. Promise me."

"Certainly," Paul said.

For Paul's sake, we carried on to the coast at a relaxed pace and arrived at Adramyttium late the next day, where we were reunited with Trimalchio.

20

Man from Macedonia

Luke insisted that Paul rest for a few days before any more travel. Trimalchio stayed with us until his master's shipment arrived and then he took it on to Troas. We arrived in Troas two days after him.

The agora was full of people from all around the Great Sea.

I'd just picked out a ripe melon and bargained a good price. As I paid the merchant, he pressed his ring into the melon's skin, leaving a clear mark embossed into its side.

"I've never seen that before," I said. "What does it mean?"

"It's my mark, to remind you who I am and that my fruit is the best. My seal of quality," he replied boastfully. "It's the Greek letter mu."

"Yes, I see. Are you Greek, then?"

"Macedonian! My family goes back to Alexander and his father Phillip. We were masters of the world! My home town is Colonia Augusta Julia Philipensis, straight across the Aegean on the Macedonian shore. It's named after the great Philip of Macedon. You may go there one day. Take this mark." He gave me a small square of cotton with his mark on it.

"God be with you," I said. I left the market, puzzled by my reaction to the Macedonian's boasting. I felt he was telling me something I needed to know, but I had no idea what.

In my dreams that night, I relived Father's stories: Paris kidnapping Helen, Odysseus and Achilles attacking Troas and failing, then hiding in a wooden horse to get into the city.

Why were we in Troas, not Bithynia or Mysia? Had the gods of Phrygia, Greece and Rome all conspired to oppose our little band with weariness and injury? Where do we go now?

I awoke confused by my dreams. I prayed for the people we'd met on the journey. I prayed especially for Cassandra, that she would know God's plan for her life, whatever that might be. It was foolish to swim against the current of his will. My mind was at rest, but my heart was devoted to Cassandra. Could such love ever be satisfied?

I caught up with the others at the baths, left my clothes in a cubicle and took towels to the poolside where Silas, Luke and Paul sat. I greeted them, then soaked my feet and calves in the water.

"My friends," Paul said, "I've been deeply troubled over the past month. Each time we moved into the enemy's territory, something prevented us. Now here we are at Asia's western limit."

He eased himself into the hot bath and rubbed his fist into his back. "My body strengthens every hour, and I long to preach. Last night in a vision, I saw a tall, strong man wearing loose, white leggings, a red sash from waist to shoulder and an embroidered shirt. Macedonian clothes! He begged me to come to Macedonia."

"Wait," I said. "I have something to show you." I rushed to the cubicle and retrieved the Macedonian's mark from my tunic.

"A merchant gave me this yesterday. He told me to take it with me if I ever went to Macedonia. I'm tired of fruitless travelling. If God is leading, let's go."

"That's the initial of Macedon," Paul said. "Confirmation!"

"There'll be trouble," Silas said. "We must be ready. The master's armour protects us: waistband of truth, breastplate of righteousness, shoes to carry the gospel of peace, shield of faith, helmet of salvation and the sword of the Spirit, God's word."

Paul gripped Silas' arm. "Well said. We're going to Macedonia, my friends."

He turned to me. "Timothy, you're like a son to me. Without you, I might still be crippled on the road from Cotyaeum. God was all wise when he chose you for his work."

"Paul, your words mean everything to me. Thank you for your trust."

"It's the master's approval you must strive for, Timothy, and I'm sure you have it. God has his hand on you, my son."

He stood in the baths, facing us. "Now, while the Spirit is at work, Silas and I will pack and arrange passage. Timothy, is your friend Trimalchio still in Troas?"

"Yes, his ship leaves tomorrow."

"Find him. He'll know how to get a ship from here. Find out what he knows and report back to me. We'll leave as soon as possible."

The day flew by while we rushed about making arrangements. We needed sailing papers which Luke obtained from the port officials. Aquius Trio, the boatmaster Trimalchio had hired to ferry his master's freight to Neapolis had space for all four of us. When I bartered with Aquius for the fare, he halved the price because Luke could serve as ship's physician and I offered to be ship's carpenter. There were repairs to the decking and railing that I could do while we sailed. When I reported this to Paul, he was full of compliments at the arrangements. It made me feel like a man, to be used in adult business. We had to sell poor Ruth, however. Aquius Trio wouldn't take her.

"Don't make no help on ship," he said. "Ain't no carpenter nor doc, so it go full price and more. Bring it or sell it. Ain't no skin off my nose, but it's pay first, I gotta tell ya, or it don't go."

So we sold her and wished her well. We'd still be at the flooded bridge without her.

We hoisted our cart onto the deck. It was packed with food and drink for the two days at sea and we had Paul's tent for shelter if we needed it. I took the wheels off the cart and lashed cart and wheels to the deckrail. Once under sail, we'd sleep on deck, just as the other passengers.

After helping us load, Trimalchio saw to his master's goods. Trimalchio would return to Cotyeaum as soon as he'd loaded his cargo and the ship sailed. This was likely the last time I'd see him.

Daylight was fading when he finished and met us on the wharf.

"My friend," I said, "God be with you. We may never meet again, but even so, I love you and will pray for you always. Safe journey."

"Tim, you and your friends are good men. Like brothers. I remember your words about Jesus. I pray to him, and to all the gods. I'll tell my master of you and of your help, so if you ever come to Cotyaeum he'll find a place for you. Farewell, my friends."

We each embraced him and bade one last farewell. I watched him walk away along the wharf. Tears welled in my eyes. It didn't seem right to let a man I'd come to love so deeply just walk away.

"Take care of him, Lord," I whispered.

Aquius Trio didn't let passengers on deck until morning, so we went to find a quiet corner of the wharf where we could sleep overnight. Many passengers huddled there, giving us safety in numbers.

While Silas was getting a meal ready, I took Paul aside. "Walk with me a little. I want to talk with you."

He stood slowly, and his first few steps were tentative. He gently rubbed his back just above his left hip.

"Paul," I said. "I've been worried about you. Has your back healed? Are you strong enough for more travel?"

"Thanks for your concern, Timothy. This week of rest and Luke's expert attention have made a great difference. There's still some pain, but I've learned how to avoid over-straining it. I'm ready."

He gained strength as we walked and there was no further sign of discomfort. I took him at his word. "I also want to ask your advice about Trimalchio," I continued. "I've failed him. He won't give up his gods and follow Jesus."

"Don't be so hard on yourself, Timothy. Not every soul we meet is going to accept the truth. God works in mysterious ways. He's not finished with Trimalchio. As long as you pray for him, the truths you've taught your friend won't be forgotten. They'll do their work."

We came to the end of the pier where Aquius Trio's ship was berthed, then turned and started back.

"Thank you, Paul. I'll keep praying. But I can't help thinking there's more I could have done."

"Maybe. With some people, you must know their greatest need. It may be a burden they want lifted, or a lack they long to fill. Let Jesus meet that need. Then they'll trust Him."

"I understand, Paul," I said. "But I can't shake my concern for Trimalchio. Let me seek him out. If I'm unsuccessful, I'll let it go."

"Very well Tiimothy, but keep your eye out for trouble. We don't know this city's dangers. We'll pray for you."

"If I find him I'll stay with him tonight and come to you in the morning," I said.

I turned quickly and started off toward some walled compounds along the wharf where Trimalchio had stored his shipment. The ships creeked and banged against the wharf and the sea lapped against the shore. A few oil lamps glowed where groups were camped and the hum of idle chatter set me at ease. I was about to enter the dark warehouse through its black hole of a doorway. Suddenly it was very quiet. The hairs on my neck stood up.

I felt a rank breath and raspy whisper, "Nary a word now or your life is o'er."

A strong blow behind my knees brought me down. From the doorway, a dark shape rushed toward me and threw itself upon my assailant. "Demon! You've got the wrong one this night!"

A knife fell to the ground. A head battered into the dust. Screams, growls, a whimper. Two shapes rose as one from the earth, then separated. One took flight, his cloak flapping behind. The other turned and staggered, then regained his footing. He steadied himself and I saw his silhouette: sleight of build, holding a knife at his side. My saviour or my death, I didn't know which. I braced for another assault, tightened into myself, blood rushing deafeningly through my veins.

"Timothy, Tim, you all right? Speak to me, my friend." The face was hidden by the dark, but not the voice.

"Trimalchio! Thank God, I'm saved. I've been looking for you and the master has provided. What happened? Where did you come from?"

"Tim, I've been watching that rascal since my shipment was moved here. That pirate was after my shipment, but saw easier pickings when you appeared. Couldn't shout to warn you without showing myself. When he took you, I attacked. Sorry I waited so long afore stopping him. You must've been frightened to death."

"I was that," I croaked, "I thought you were his accomplice and I was done for. I owe you my life, Trimalchio." I paused for breath then embraced him in a great hug. "Thank you, my friend, but when I need rescuing, let me be part of it. You had all the fun. Don't leave me out next time."

He laughed. "I'll keep that in mind, Tim. But are you mad, walking the wharf alone in the dark? It's dangerous here."

"I was looking for you. I couldn't rest tonight until I had one last chance to talk with you."

"Well then, let's get into my haven. It ain't fancy, but I've sparked a little fire on the floor and was near to roasting some fish. Hungry?"

We walked through the warehouse doors, now a welcoming sanctuary. I saw his fire in a far corner. Other warehousemen had set themselves to guard various parts of the building. Now I understood why my assailant attacked me outside rather than raid the warehouse. It would take several men to overcome these guards, but only one to defeat me. We sat before Trimalchio's fire while he skewered two fresh fish and set about roasting them. He drew a serving of wine from an amphora and bent over, gazing into the flames.

"I keep to myself on these trips, Timothy. There's danger along interior roads. Not a safe place for lone travellers. I've seen some horrible things, horrible things, my friend."

I didn't reply. I'd seen some terrible things myself. Paul and Barnabas beaten, Rachel scarred, Marius' home destroyed and Marius himself nearly killed. All restored by the grace of God. Trimalchio's voice was heavy with resignation and pessimism. I remembered Paul's advice and asked my friend to tell me more. Maybe his stories would reveal his need.

He reached for a fish just as it was about to fall off the spit, gave it to me and took the other for himself. He picked at the flesh and said, "Tim, have you ever done something you're ashamed of?"

He spoke casually, but I took it seriously, though I didn't know where he was about to go with this gloomy question.

"Because I have," he continued, swallowing a morsel and pausing to collect his thoughts.

I wasn't ready to share my failures and was relieved he didn't wait for my answer. "You've got my attention, Trimalchio. Tell me more."

He stared into the fire as if to search out its purifying power.

"It was awful, my friend." He turned and stirred the fire with a stick.

His voice broke as he continued. "I've told no one, and it can't be fixed. I'm haunted by it at night, when I'm alone. Frightened awake by nightmares, I am. Can't be fixed," he repeated. He tried to swallow the sob that broke from his soul.

"Maybe it can, Trimalchio. Would you fix it if it you could?"

"Ay, 'course I would. If I could keep my standing. I'm a slave, Tim, but I'm trusted in my master's house. It can't be fixed," he sighed. "And my life's ruined, if the truth be told. I'm afraid the dreadful secret will kill me by a thousand strokes. What am I to do?"

I prayed for wisdom. It was clear to me that Trimalchio needed to be cleansed from the guilt he so keenly felt. I was sure he would embrace God's forgiveness. The question was, would he do so if it cost him his reputation and livelihood?

"Trimalchio, there is forgiveness in Christ's work. Tell your sin and his grace will save you."

"I can't, Tim. You're my friend. You'd not be if you knew this."

"Not so, Trimalchio, I'll always be your friend. After tonight we may never see one another again. What you tell me is our secret. I won't tell a soul, but you must let the master deal with it. There may be consequences for your deeds, payments to be made, apologies, but you'll be freed from the guilt. Whatever happens, whatever punishment, it won't imprison you. Your spirit will soar with the Spirit of God."

"Can that be true? But I'm imprisoned now with this heavy guilt and shame. What could be worse?"

He sighed and began his story.

"Tim, I'm a murderer. I beat and killed a man years ago. Met him on the road I did, while traveling for my master. Walked together. Shared my food. Talked together on the road and at night. Morning, I caught him reaching into my bag, stealing my purse. I was enraged. Betrayal of friendship. It weren't the money, 'twas the betrayal. I beat him senseless. Dragged him to the thick trees. Covered him so he couldn't be seen from the road.

"He was dead. I left him for the wild critters to tear apart. Tried to clear my guilt. 'He's a thief, unknown, not be missed,' I told myself. 'World was better without him. I'd rescued future victims from his treachery.' All true, but none of it's taken away my guilt. I felt the same rage tonight when I attacked the pirate. If you weren't there, I'd have killed him. What can I do?"

I was thinking of how easy it is, when you know Christ, to bare your soul to him. Trimalchio knew the gods as vindictive and unpredictable. He had no framework to understand a forgiving God.

"Trimalchio, my friend, God forgives you if you agree with Him that this evil thing is wrong. Confess it and follow Jesus from now on."

Trimalchio moved back from the fire, bent over, placed his head to the floor and wept as he spoke. "Forgive me, God. I don't deserve your grace. Free me from the guilt and shame of my murderous actions. I turn to you and you alone, Master."

When he lifted his face the firelight revealed the tears on his cheeks and his eyes alive with joy. I had heard the words I longed to hear from this brave, tortured soul: "You and you alone, Master."

We spent much of the night talking about the truth. Shades of darkness lifted from his eyes. Everything I told him made sense once he'd accepted God's unconditional love. Love that contrasted so strongly with the capricious nature of his gods. By dawn his only remaining question was, "What of the man I killed? What do I do about him?"

"Are you still afraid of what might happen to you, Trimalchio?" I asked.

"No," he stated firmly. "I'm right with God. What can man do to me?"

"Then this is what you must do. First, tell your master what you've told me. Tell exactly what happened, that he was stealing from you. Have him report the killing to the authorities. They'll investigate and may arrest you, but if your master goes with you they'll treat you properly according to the law. His influence may prevent any punishment. The man you murdered was, after all, a common thief. You were protecting your master's property."

First light broke and Trimalchio snuffed the fire. He took his bag and slung it over his shoulder.

We stood on the wharf where I'd been attacked. He faced me and smiled, but his eyes still held fear. At least I'd assured him that he may not have to suffer in prison or pay with his life.

"My friend," I said. "Remember the words of Jesus: 'I'm with you always, to the very end of the age.' His presence will keep you from fear."

He embraced me and shook my hand, then smiled widely. "Whoop Timothy!" he shouted. "I'll see you in Cotyaeum, my friend." He turned and ran away along the wharf.

"God be with you!" I yelled back, and he waved one arm over his head as he sped along the way home.

I stood in awe of the Spirit's leadership and protection. I left Trimalchio knowing he was safe in God's hands and prayed we'd meet again.

I walked back to meet my friends. Paul, Silas and Luke were relieved to see me and rejoiced at the work of God that night. They'd prayed for the first hour after I left them. Then they felt the peace of God and slept well until morning.

"Paul," I said, "it was dangerous, like you said it would be."

"Yes," he answered, "but we must engage the enemy whatever the circumstances, Timothy. The Spirit burdened you with your friend's eternal destiny. I knew God would be with you throughout this. He's been with you from the start. One must not resist the Spirit. You've conquered your fear and are strengthened by the master's courage."

We had a few hours before setting sail. I walked to a green hillside overlooking the Aegean's crystal clear, blue-green waters. I prayed, remembering friends I'd met on our journey. Orestes, new-born in Christ. Had he been strengthened in faith or was he still confused about circumcision and the cult of Kybele? Had Appion succeeded in bringing peace between Christians and Judeans? Had he and Cassandra married? Did my love for Cassandra have any hope against such powers? I held Cassandra's fibulae in my hand and tried to convince myself that it was God's will for us to be united one day, but even prayer wouldn't remove the doubt. I admired the fine work, the cat ever ready to pounce on the bird.

I gazed on the waters before me. Prayer hadn't cleared my mind of all fear, but as I watched the waves cleanse the shore of its flotsam, my spirit gradually refreshed as though a washing were occurring there, too. I sprang to my feet and raced the wind along the shore, kicking up wet sand and leaving tracks behind, stretching farther and farther. The more I ran, the clearer and more settled my mind became.

I remembered the boy I'd been in Lystra, how I loved exploring the countryside near my home. There was endless variety to the caves, rocks, and hills of my homeland. I'd test myself there, running along the paths and up the slopes until I was exhausted. Then I'd stop, gasping until I could breathe again, finally to retrace my steps down the hillside and to home.

Here on the Aegean beach, just as I'd done in Lystra, I stopped running when my breath gave out. I looked back as far as I could see.

There in the distance was our ship and, nearer, my tracks on the shore. I had come much farther than I realized.

CPSIA information can be obtained
at www.ICGtesting.com
Printed in the USA
LVOW04s2312250416
485288LV00013B/61/P